BOSS MAN

BOSS #2

VICTORIA QUINN

Hartwick Publishing

Boss Man

1

TITAN

WE CHECKED in to our resort, a breathtaking place situated in the rock crevasse overlooking the beautiful Mediterranean Sea. The sun had just gone down, and the soft colors of the sky were slowly fading away as night deepened. I'd been here several times, mostly for business, and it was a place embedded in my heart.

I had a private balcony that opened up to a patio with a couple of lounge chairs. A bottle of champagne was there to greet me, chilled in a bucket of ice. I asked for the nicest room they had, even if I didn't need a two-bedroom suite.

As a businesswoman, I always had to protect my image.

I didn't settle for less than the best. I reminded everyone around me exactly what I was worth. While an image had no physical form, it was a barrier most people were too intimidated to cross. It stopped insulting offers from grazing across my desk.

It made people take me seriously. Even though I was the wealthiest woman in the world, I was still trying to earn the respect of every man around me. I had to work twice as hard for their admiration. One false move, and I was ridiculed in a way a man never was.

Hunt never treated me that way—it was one of the things I loved about him. I never felt like second-best. He didn't patronize me with knowledge he considered superior to my own. The only time he overstepped his boundary was when I was driving on that racetrack—and his concern wasn't inappropriate.

A knock sounded on my door.

I was pulling out my laptop from my bag, so I called over my shoulder, "It's open." I set my laptop on the desk along with my folders, knowing I was going to be taking care of business in the middle of the night since it was daytime back in Manhattan.

The door opened and closed, and heavy footsteps sounded behind me.

Only Hunt would walk inside and not say a single word to me. "How do you like your room?" I asked.

He came up behind me, pressing his concrete chest to my back. He circled my waist with his arms and held me against him as he kissed my neck and breathed into my ear. His large hands were so big and masculine, covered with thick veins all the way up his forearms. He had the kind of strength that made me feel small—and no man ever made me feel small. He squeezed me harder as he kissed me.

Now all my thoughts seized—except the ones about him.

He yanked my dress up to my waist and pulled my panties to my knees. The sound of his belt coming undone and his slacks dropping filled my ears.

I couldn't think straight because his power stole my focus. This man made me fall prey to my own carnal desires. All I could think about was his big dick inside me, that throbbing cock that did the most wonderful things to me. Hunt was exclusively mine, and he only had one purpose.

To please me.

He rubbed his dick in the crack between my cheeks, moving his arm across my chest to get a tighter grip on me. He wanted to fuck me hard. I could feel it in his tremors, in the excitement of his breaths.

I gripped his hips behind me and held on to his arm for balance. The more he wanted me, the more desirable I felt. He was one of the most handsome men I'd ever seen, with his dark eyes and matching exterior. My dreams were always full of him, the man who seduced me in a way no one else ever had. "Hunt...fuck me." I couldn't wait any longer. He brought me from zero to sixty in zero seconds.

"Yes, Boss Lady." Just when he was about to point his cock inside me, my phone rang.

It was sitting on the desk, so we could see the name on the screen.

Brett.

What the hell did he want? We were just on a plane together for eight hours.

Hunt saw it but obviously didn't care. He gripped me tighter and placed his head inside me.

Just that bit of a stretching made me gasp. My nails dug into his forearms, and my nipples hardened against his arm.

A knock sounded on the door.

Hunt stopped moving, his breathing silenced.

God fucking dammit.

"It's Brett," he said. "Wanted to see if you wanted to get dinner."

Hunt growled against my ear, all his hatred expressed in the single, guttural sound. His phone started to vibrate in his pocket when someone called him, and we both knew it was Brett.

Hunt stepped back and quickly pulled his clothes back on. He tucked in his shirt and controlled his breathing, trying to appear as calm as possible—not like a man who was just about to get laid.

I pulled up my panties and yanked my dress down. It only took two seconds to get ready, so I walked to the door and answered. "Hey."

"Hey." His phone was pressed to his ear as he continued to call Hunt. He hung up and stowed the phone in his pocket. "Wanted to see if you guys wanted to get dinner. I've looked for Hunt, but I'm not sure where he ran off to."

He was about to run off deep inside me before we were interrupted. "We were just standing on the patio having a glass of champagne." I opened the door wider, revealing Hunt in the background taking in the view. He had a glass of the golden liquid in his hand.

"It's a beautiful place—and worth celebrating." He welcomed himself inside and didn't think twice about the fact that Hunt and I were alone together in my room.

Since the world thought I was dating Thorn, it usually stopped people from being suspicious of the other men I spent time with. "Where should we have dinner?" I closed the door behind him, and we all walked outside to the patio. The sky was darkening, the refracted rays of the sun long gone.

Hunt looked at me, his expression calm, like nothing had happened. But his eyes told a very different story. He wanted to strangle his brother to death—I could tell.

"There's a good place here at the resort," Brett said. "I thought we could have a nice meal then try to get some sleep before the shoot tomorrow."

I'd already slept on the plane, so I wouldn't be able to sleep tonight. I never adjusted to changing time zones, so I operated on my own schedule. Besides, I had a few phone calls to make. "Sounds good to me."

Hunt downed the rest of his glass. "Let's do it."

WE HAD A TABLE ON THE TERRACE, UNDER A STREAM OF white lights. Couples sat at other tables, obviously on honeymoons. There were very few business partners together since this place was more for vacations rather than professional meetings.

Our plates were nearly wiped clean, and we'd gone through two bottles of wine. Hunt and I hadn't started our arrangement too long ago, but it seemed to be working perfectly. He didn't stare at me openly like he did when it was just the two of us. He appeared indifferent toward me, like he wasn't attracted to me at all.

I appreciated it.

Brett turned to me, with the same deep brown eyes

Hunt possessed. Brett was older, and he appeared a little more rugged than Hunt. They didn't look like half-brothers, but full brothers. He retained the exact same confidence, along with a splash of arrogance. "Titan, will Thorn be joining us for the trip?"

Thorn was in Chicago, handling one of the head-quarters for his thriving business. His family was the exclusive owners of the biggest tomato factory in the world. It'd been handed down for generations, landing in Thorn's lap. But he took his fortune and invested it into other companies, bringing him to a new level of wealth that his family could never have dreamed of. I never saw him make a mistake. When he planned for his future endeavors, he saw it as a marathon—never a sprint. I learned a lot from him. Actually, I learned everything from him. If he hadn't walked into that bar when I was nineteen years old, I wouldn't be where I was now.

I owed him everything.

Hunt turned his gaze my way, watching my reaction to the question.

"No. He's very busy in Chicago right now."

Brett gave a slight nod. "He bought one of my cars about a year ago."

"He told me," I answered. "He took me for a drive a few times. That's exactly why I bought one for myself."

Brett smiled. "Awesome. Free publicity."

Even now, I didn't confirm or deny that Thorn and I were together. But when people made assumptions, I didn't correct them. It was all part of our plan, our future. Hunt had asked me several questions about it, but since it was none of his business, I never gave an answer—and I wasn't going to. "What about you, Brett? Have anyone special in your life?"

"I have many special women," he answered. "But they all come and go."

I didn't expect anything less from a handsome man such as himself. He was wealthy, smart, and had amazing looks. He could play the field as long as he wanted. When he turned fifty, he could still land a woman half his age and start a family if he wanted to.

I didn't have that kind of luxury.

I had a ticking time bomb on my uterus.

"What about you?" Brett turned to Hunt. "Any more threesomes?"

I knew Hunt was the kind of man who could get any woman he wanted—and as many of them as he wanted. The lust I felt between my legs was echoed by every other woman on the planet. But for now, I didn't have to share him.

He was all mine.

Hunt took the question in stride. "I don't think that's

appropriate conversation in front of a lady."

I rolled my eyes. "I'm not a lady—just a business associate. And as you two must know, women love sex too." Some women would be turned off by Hunt's promiscuity, even jealous. But I thought that kind of endurance was sexy, pleasing two women at once was an incredible feat.

But I already knew he was good at it—based on experience.

Brett smiled at me, the affection in his eyes. "I'll drink to that." He held up his glass.

I clinked mine against his before I took a drink.

Hunt watched me, his eyes hardening the way they did when we were alone together.

I purposely looked away, reminding him that we were just associates when we weren't fucking—and friends.

"The crew will meet us just a drive down the road," Brett said. "All the permits have been taken care of, but we have to get the footage as quickly as possible. The government is only allowing us to block traffic for one hour."

"Shouldn't be a problem," Hunt said. "We can get it on the first take."

"I don't need to remind you how valuable these cars are," Brett said. "But more importantly, you guys need to stay safe. I would hate to have one of you drive over the cliff and to the bottom of the ocean."

"We'll be fine." I dismissed his concern immediately, knowing I could drive perfectly well.

When Hunt looked at me, he showed a hint of concern.

I ignored it, not needing a man to worry over my well-being.

WHEN I GOT BACK TO THE ROOM, I TOOK CARE OF A FEW emails and spoke to Jessica on the phone. She assured me everything was going well at the office, running so smoothly that people didn't even realize I wasn't there.

I expected Hunt to come by the room to pick up where he left off, but judging by the kind of businessman he was, he was doing the exact same thing I was doing.

When the thought of his naked body came to mind, I texted him. *Come to my room. Now.* I loved getting exactly what I wanted, when I wanted it. The tables would turn in a short time and I'd be the one to obey, but I tried not to think about it.

I just focused on now.

He knocked on my door minutes later, dressed in

sweatpants and a t-shirt. Whether he was dressed in a suit or nothing at all, he looked incredible. His pants were low on his hips, and his t-shirt stretched across his powerful chest. The second the door was open, he walked inside, staying out of the hallway so he wouldn't be seen by anyone.

I was already naked, not wanting to waste time with clothes.

His eyes went straight to my tits. "We should be careful, Titan. If my brother stops by my room and I'm not there..."

"Just tell him you met someone. Problem solved." I walked out of the room and to the back patio. I had a private pool that faced the water, and since no one was around at this time of night, it seemed like the entire city belonged to me.

Hunt followed me outside, his shirt gone.

I stepped down the stairs that led into the water, feeling the cold against my skin. When the water was to my shoulders, I turned around and looked at him.

Still as a statue, he watched me glide in the water. His eyes followed me everywhere I went, and the slight waves reflected across his wide chest. His narrow waist was lined with abs, the sides of his torso a thick stretch of muscle. He was chiseled in ways I'd never seen on other men. He was lean and toned, but so ripped each muscle stood out. Whenever we shared a meal together, he always picked healthy options. It definitely paid off.

"Get in."

Hunt had several different kinds of smiles, and they all meant very different things. Sometimes he smiled wide, his public persona for the cameras. Other times, he smiled slightly, like his body felt the urge to smile even if he didn't want to. Then there was how he smiled at me now, unable to hold back his amusement.

He pulled his sweatpants and boxers off, revealing the enormous cock I was completely smitten with. Then he took the stairs into the water, drops splashing onto his chest and arms. Since he was much taller than me, his shoulders and chest stayed above the waterline when I was mostly submerged.

My body ached to finish what we started before dinner. He would have fucked me so good, right against my desk with his powerful grip around my chest. I loved being squeezed with those big hands, watching the veins in his forearms bulge with blood from the constriction of his strong muscles.

Diesel Hunt was the biggest weakness I'd ever known, the best sex I'd ever had. I'd been with incredible men who knew how to make me feel good, but none of them compared to this very talented man.

I loved his power.

His smile.

And I loved how he made me feel like a woman.

He grabbed my hips and guided me until I straddled him, my weight nonexistent because of the buoyancy of the water. I pretty much floated there as he directed me with his hands. He guided me into deeper water then pressed me against a wall, his powerful body and strong hands keeping me in place.

He ground his cock against my folds in the water, his nose rubbing against mine. The water was cold, but his skin was still searing hot. I could feel it when I touched him. My arms locked around his neck, and I kissed the corner of his mouth, slowing down our intensity.

His fingers kneaded my ass as he kissed me, squeezing both of my cheeks with his iron grip before releasing them. His mouth brushed against mine before he pulled back again, taking the opportunity to look at me, my hair floating in the water. "How do you want me to please you, Boss Lady?" His deep voice was sexy, like masculinity rubbing against sandpaper. His chin was covered in hair because he hadn't had a chance to shave since we left New York, and he rubbed it against me every time he dragged his mouth against mine. He was one of the most recognizable men in the business world, one of the elite who graced the cover of magazines just for stepping outside his penthouse. He was a leader, not a follower. But he wanted to conquer me so much that he was willing to let himself be conquered first.

I'd never witnessed anything sexier.

I had this man under my thumb. He was my toy, my plaything. I could do whatever I wanted to him—and he would enjoy it.

"I want it slow."

He positioned his cock at my entrance and slowly pushed inside.

My nails dug into his shoulders, and I breathed against his mouth, my entire body tightening as he moved inside me. "I want it deep."

He sheathed himself until he was balls deep, his coffee eyes trained on me. He watched my reaction, his face hard as steel and giving nothing in return. He pressed his entire body against me, crowding me against the wall, pinning me down so I had nowhere else to go.

"I want you to come inside me as many times as you can...and not stop until I say so."

His mouth was slightly parted against mine when he moaned quietly. He was buried deep between my legs, so far inside there was nowhere else to go. His heated desire made him impressively thick, thicker than he'd ever been before.

I used my grip on his shoulders to move myself into him, to pull his cock out and take it in again.

He pushed me against the wall, halting my movements, and started to move. He made long and exaggerated thrusts, dragging them out so they were slow like I wanted.

I almost told him to step back, but it felt too good. A gorgeous man was fucking me nice and steady, hitting me in the perfect spot with every single thrust.

"Fuck, you're beautiful." He gripped my wet hair in his fist and kissed me, driving his tongue into my mouth without interrupting his regular thrusts. He breathed hard into my mouth between kisses, but the passion never halted. When we were together like this, I didn't think about the office. I didn't think about my friends. I didn't think about anything else going on in my life. It was pure heat, pure lust. It was the best distraction I'd ever known—even more powerful than a dozen Old Fashioneds.

I gripped his lower back and guided him into me, gripping his powerful body just so I had something to hold on to. My thighs squeezed his waist over and over because I knew exactly what was coming. It was a volcanic eruption between my legs, so searingly hot and powerful. "Hunt…"

He sealed his mouth over mine to muffle my screams. I wouldn't want anyone to overhear us and complain to the front desk. Brett could easily connect

two and two together and draw the kind of conclusions I
didn't need.

Hunt did a great job keeping me quiet, used to the
way I came because we'd fucked so many times now.
When my screams turned particularly violent, he gave
me his tongue and took mine as hostage, forcing me to
move with him and keep my silence.

But the climax was so good. I was still throbbing
even when it passed. My fingers dug into Hunt's skin,
and I felt a strong wave of affection for this man, hailing
him as a god for doing these incredible things to me.

He pressed his forehead to mine when I was
finished, catching his breath as he continued to push me
against the wall over and over again.

"Your turn." I gripped his ass and pulled him deep
into me, getting as much of his length as would fit
before he hit my cervix. "I want it, Hunt. I want all of it."

He groaned as he pushed harder into me.

"And I want you to say my name as you finish—
Titan. Eyes on me." I wanted to watch him climax, watch
him come deep inside my pussy so I would always
remember it. I wanted to watch him come undone, for
his breathing to pause just before he took a deep breath
as he released. I wanted to feel all of his muscles tighten
for me, his cock throb as it released mounds of his seed
—just for me.

He thrust a little harder, moving his body through the resistance of the water. My back hit the wall repeatedly as he thrust, his hands holding my folded body against him. He kept his hard gaze focused on me, those deep brown eyes looking darker than usual. His jaw was slowly tightening like a screw turning inside a hole.

When he closed his eyes for an instant, I knew he'd hit his trigger. He suddenly thrust harder into me, moving into his climax. The water swished around us, lapping up against the sides from his momentum. "Titan..." He pinned me against him, his ass tight as hell, and he released with a moan. Not once did he close his eyes, his scorching gaze trained on mine. His cock throbbed deep inside me as he dumped all of his come inside my aching pussy.

I moaned when I felt his warm stickiness fill my channel. It was heavy and good, full of Hunt's powerful desire for me.

His cock slowly softened inside me when he finished, but he kept himself buried between my legs. I wasn't finished with him yet, and he knew that. His hand moved back into my hair, and he started to kiss me, slowly. He built his arousal back up, knowing he needed to get hard for me so he could give me more of his come.

Because I wanted all of it—every last drop.

2

HUNT

THE SCENE WAS SET up and ready to shoot. The cars were already on, ready to go. They were convertibles, a different model than the versions Titan and I drove. Our plan was to drive down the coast one-quarter of a mile. She was supposed to cut me off, wearing a smile as she did it. I was to catch up to her in the opposite lane, and we were going to share a long look.

It was pretty simple.

But I was worried. The only thing beside the road was the cliff face. One wrong move, and the car could plummet to its demise.

I wasn't worried about me—I was worried about her.

One thing I learned about Titan was she knew how to take care of herself. She was wickedly smart and confident. She'd obviously learned life lessons the hard way. There was no other explanation as to why she was so hard—like steel. She didn't need me to be concerned about her. She didn't even need me to care about her.

But I did.

"There's still time to use a stunt double," I said to both Brett and Titan thirty minutes before sunset. The weather was perfect, a clear sky with plenty of heat. We didn't have much time left before the cameras started rolling, but the actors would come out immediately for the right price.

"No doubles," Titan said. "We'll be fine."

I didn't challenge her in front of Brett, but I wished I were the one in charge. If I were, I would tell her we would use doubles—and she'd have to suck it up. "No one will even know."

"Yes, they will," Titan said. "It's so obvious every time I watch a car commercial. We can handle it, Hunt."

Brett watched her with obvious affection, respecting Titan more than he respected most people. "If that's what the woman wants, that's what she gets."

I wanted to strangle my brother. This would be so much easier if I just told him the truth. It was becoming more tempting to break my promise to Titan. It's not like she would know about it. But my pride in my word stopped me. If she didn't trust me, then she would call off our arrangement.

"Get into the cars, and we'll do the first take." Brett

talked to the director, who was still setting up the final touches on the cameras.

Titan walked to her car, wearing a white blouse with a blue scarf tied around her neck. When professionals did her hair and makeup, she looked like she belonged on the front cover of a magazine. If business wasn't her thing, hitting the runway could have been a strong second choice.

I came up behind her and grabbed her by the elbow.

She immediately pulled her arm away, taking another step to the right to keep us far apart. "Don't touch me in public, Hunt." She lacked the venom of someone who was angry, saying the words with pure simplicity.

I almost grabbed her again anyway—for the hell of it. "Titan, I don't know about this."

"Hunt, you're overreacting."

"You aren't a professional driver."

"Neither are you," she countered.

"But your life is a lot more important than mine."

She stopped when she reached the car and gave me a different kind of look. She glanced to the right to look at the crew members before she looked at me again. "I don't see why."

I didn't have a reason either. All I knew was, I didn't want her to get hurt. If something happened to me, then whatever. But if something happened to her...it would haunt me every single day of my life. Titan wasn't just my friend, but someone I'd come to respect. I cared about her a lot, more than I cared about most people. "You represent hope, equality, and respect for a lot of people. You may be the most powerful woman in the world, but you aren't invincible. The world can't afford to lose you."

She sighed as she looked at me, frustrated and touched. "That's a sweet thing to say, Hunt. I appreciate it. But I still think you're overreacting. We're going to shoot a few takes and then move on with our lives."

I hated not having control. I fucking hated it. If she were mine right now, all I'd have to say was no.

Six weeks couldn't come quick enough.

She stepped closer to me, returning the proximity she took away. Her bright eyes looked into mine, wearing the expression I'd seen dozens of times. She gave it right before she kissed me, pressed a soft kiss to my mouth.

If we were alone, she'd be kissing me now.

"Please be careful." I tried getting through to her, but it obviously didn't make a difference. Cars like these contained more horsepower than a semitruck. While they were collectibles, they weren't meant to be toys.

Her eyes softened slightly, the first time I'd ever seen them react that way. "I will, Hunt."

WE FINISHED SHOOTING AN HOUR LATER, JUST AS THE SUN dipped below the horizon. We got the shots, and the work was complete.

It went as smoothly as planned.

Once the cars were returned and we were back on foot, I felt the tightness in my stomach disappear at last. The nausea went away, and I could finally stand tall without the heavy weight on my shoulders.

Brett walked up to me once he was finished talking to the director. "You alright, man? You look a little pale."

"I'm fine." I watched Titan hand over the keys to her car and speak to one of the crew members. He said something to make her laugh. Then she wore her diplomatic smile, being polite even though she didn't really care about the conversation. I'd seen that look enough times to know exactly what it meant.

Brett followed my gaze before he looked at me again. "Still haunts you?"

"Sometimes."

He clapped me on the shoulder and gave me a

sympathetic look. "I'm sorry, man. But you know better than anyone that I know exactly how you feel."

I nodded. "I know."

He dropped his hand and continued to stand beside me. "You like Titan, don't you?"

My eyes landed on his when I heard what he said, looking into the brown eyes so similar to my own. He was only older than me by two years, but I'd always looked up to him as someone so much wiser. He was good at reading people—even me. "Why do you ask that?"

"You've acted this way twice now—both times she's been in a car."

Perhaps I'd made it more obvious than I meant to. "I care about her...but that's it."

Brett narrowed his eyes incredulously, not buying my excuse. "Come on, remember who you're talking to."

I avoided his gaze, feeling like a specimen under a microscope. "It doesn't matter how I feel about her. She's seeing Thorn. Let's stop talking about it." I felt like shit not telling him the truth, that I was bedding her. Nothing would ever come of it because it was just physical, but I'd never been monogamous with anyone in my life. Felt strange not to tell him. It was a big part of my life.

Brett backed off when he knew I wasn't going to say

anymore. "Alright. I heard you loud and clear." He walked back to the director where Titan was now standing. They exchanged a few words and then handshakes.

Once the shoot was wrapped up, we headed back to the resort.

BRETT AND I WENT OUT THAT NIGHT, AND I DIDN'T HAVE A legitimate excuse to say no. I told him I wasn't seeing anyone, and since I always went out and picked up women, it didn't make sense to say no.

Especially when he was catching on to my attraction to Titan.

We went to a club an hour down the coast, taking one of his cars to get there. I never told Titan I was leaving because I wasn't in the mood to talk to her. My brother's comment about my concern for her irritated me.

I shouldn't care this much about her.

In my gut, I knew it wasn't just because I was sleeping with her, that it wasn't just because I wanted to fuck her as long as I could. Ever since I saw her handle those sexist comments, I'd come to respect her. She had a brilliant mind and a beautiful face. She was different from the rest, only pretending to be cold and hard because that's what the world turned her into.

I knew there was more underneath.

There was a connection between us that was stronger than sex.

I actually liked her.

Titan texted me on the drive, her message popping up on my screen. Thankfully, Brett's eyes were on the road, so he didn't notice. *I want you.* Her tone was so bossy, even through a text message. I could hear her voice in my head as I read the words. I'd much rather be buried deep between her legs than out with my brother pretending to catch some tail. *Come to my room in ten minutes.*

I can't. I'm out with Brett.

How is that my problem?

I smiled automatically, loving her no-bullshit attitude. I assumed allowing someone to speak to me that way would annoy me, but it was just a turn-on. What kind of man didn't love hearing how much a woman wanted him? Especially the most powerful woman on the planet? *I'm an hour away. We're going to a club.*

Then come by when you're done.

I doubt you'll be awake.

Try me.

Man, she really wanted me. *I'm gonna have to pretend to hook up with someone. Brett is growing suspicious of us.*

Her message popped up immediately. *We'll discuss this later.*

I couldn't stop my fingers from typing the message. *Yes, Boss Lady.*

Come by my room. I don't care what time it is. I slipped my room key into your wallet.

My eyebrows furrowed, trying to think of a time when I left my wallet unattended. *When did you do that?*

When you were putting your pants back on.

A PRETTY BRUNETTE STUCK TO MY SIDE THE WHOLE NIGHT, and I rested my arm over her shoulders. She turned into me and kissed me on the neck then nibbled on my earlobe.

I wasn't doing anything wrong, just putting on an act, but I didn't like it. I hated pretending to be interested in this woman, wasting her time, and leading her on. She kept gripping my thigh and tugging on my jeans, wanting to get my pants off.

How much longer did I have to do this?

Did Titan really expect me to do this for three months?

When I looked at Brett, he was making out with a blonde, pinning her into the couch with her leg around his waist. They were pretty much having sex with their clothes on.

His car was a two-seater, so I had the perfect excuse to get out of there.

I said goodbye to the brunette and called the hotel to get a ride. Even if my date for the evening told Brett I ditched her, I could just say I took someone else back to the room instead. It sounded like something I would do anyway.

The car picked me up and drove me back to the resort. It was a long drive, and my thoughts drifted to Titan. I hoped she was still awake, sleeping in just her panties. I had no idea how she slept because I'd never witnessed it, so I let my imagination pull a picture together.

When I arrived at the hotel, I went to her room and let myself inside.

It was three in the morning—and she was still awake.

She paced in the luxurious living room with the phone pressed to her ear. She was speaking to someone in her office. "Reschedule that meeting. Yes. For Friday. And I have a few things that need to be picked up from the dry cleaners. I'll call back if I need anything else,

Jessica." She ended the call and turned around. She didn't seem startled to see me standing there, so she must have heard the door shut from the other side of the hotel room. "How was your evening?"

"Shitty."

"How so?" She walked to her private bar and poured two Old Fashioneds. I assumed one was for me, but with Titan, there was no way to tell.

"Brett stuck his tongue down some woman's throat, while another tried to rip my pants off."

She sauntered toward me, dressed in a short black dress with no shoes on. She placed the glass in my hand before she took a drink of her own. "I can't say I blame her. I would have done the same thing." She sat on the couch and crossed her legs, her dress hiking up. It must have been a nightgown because it seemed too scandalous to wear in public.

I took a seat on the couch across from her, letting my legs fall open as I held the glass on my thigh. She still had her makeup on even though it was late in the evening. I'd never seen her without makeup before. The most casual I'd seen her was in jeans—and they weren't that casual.

I was screwing this woman, but I still didn't really know her.

My other flings had been shorter, but at least I knew

something about them. We talked before and after sex, and I learned about their lives and their families. But with Titan, we really didn't talk about anything at all.

"Do you ever sleep, Titan?" She was always going a million miles an hour, working hard during the day, partying with her friends, and keeping her place as clean as a hotel room at the Four Seasons. Did she ever relax?

She drank from her glass and glanced outside the large window that overlooked the ocean. Her curls from that afternoon had slowly softened, making her hair appear straight again. But it retained its lustrous soft-ness. There was a slight tint of red to it, only noticeable when she was directly under the sun. Her nails were painted black, something she must have done before we left for our trip. And every time I'd seen her naked, she was perfectly smooth. She must get a Brazilian wax every few weeks. She turned back to me, as if she'd finished pondering the question. "Not often, no."

She'd taken all that time to compose her answer, but she gave me a very small response. "Insomniac?"

"No, not really," she said. "I just don't like sleeping."

"You don't like it?" I brought the glass to my lips and took a drink.

"I see it as a waste of time."

I didn't sleep as much as the average person, getting

about seven hours per night. But I still needed a decent chunk of time to function, to make good decisions on a daily basis. "I disagree."

"In that amount of time, I could get so much more done."

"But you can't work all the time." I was a workaholic, fiercely ambitious, and it was a strong statement for me to make that comment to someone else. I wanted to be the richest man in the world, but I wasn't quite there. I had a few people to bump off before I took the number one spot.

"I don't work all the time."

"Then what do you do?"

She finished the contents of her glass before setting it on the coffee table. "Read. Write. Watch TV. Enjoy my alone time."

She was a regular person just like everyone else, but she said something that caught my attention. "You write?"

She broke eye contact and pulled her legs toward her body. "Well, I try."

Was this why she owned a dying publishing house? Because she loved the subject? It would explain why she preferred to lose money every quarter than let it be sold to someone else. It must be a passion of hers. "What do you write?"

"I tried writing poems, but I'm just not good at it. So, I write short stories. I've never written a full novel. Every time I try, the story dries up, and I give up."

Of all the things Titan was, I never expected her to be a writer. "That's really cool."

Her eyes searched my face like we were in a board meeting, trying to figure out if I was just saying what she wanted to hear or blowing smoke up her ass. When she saw the sincerity in my eyes, she didn't look so threatened. "You think so?" It was the first time she showed me uncertainty, relying on my opinion for validation. She didn't seem to care about my opinion of her. She didn't care what anyone thought of her. But this was one exception she seemed to make.

"Yeah. I'd love to read something—if you're ever willing to show me."

"Are you a reader?"

"I read about two books a year. Not sure if that makes me a reader or not."

"What do you like to read?" she asked.

"Thrillers. Mysterious, James Bond type of stuff."

She nodded. "Great genre."

"What genre is your work?"

She considered the question, pressing her lips tightly together before she answered. "I suppose fiction or literature. But I can't put any of my stories in a genre because I've never finished anything."

"Who says you can't finish it now?"

Now Titan didn't look like the woman I was used to seeing. She wasn't the ambitious shark that circled her prey. She was a soft woman, with beautiful cheeks and dazzling eyes. She smiled at my words, obviously valuing what I said. "It's never too late, I suppose..."

"Never." I abandoned my drink on the table and joined her on the couch. I sat right against her and positioned her leg around my waist, just the way Brett had been with his date at the club. I moved over her, slowly positioning her back against the couch.

She allowed me to guide her, her hand moving up my chest.

"All night, I wished I were back here with you." My hand pulled her dress up to her waist, revealing her bare bottom. She was commando, obviously ready for me the second I'd walked in the door.

She undid my jeans and pushed them down, along with my boxers. "I've been waiting for you..."

I positioned myself on top of her so my cock could slide right in. "I don't want to keep lying, Titan. I don't want to sit in a bar when I don't give a damn about anyone there. When my brother asks if I'm into you, I want to tell him I'm fucking you, and it's the best sex I've ever had. I want to be real."

She cupped my face and kissed me, her lips so soft against my mouth. She breathed into me before she grabbed my hips and slowly tugged me deep inside. "I know, but I won't change my mind. If this is too difficult, then we should both walk away."

Now that I was deep inside her pussy, I couldn't think straight. I was inhaling her scent, loving the smell of vanilla as well as her arousal. When I was inside her, it felt like the only place I should be. My face was close to hers, and I could feel her breathe, feel her warm breath fall on my skin. Her fingers dug into me, begging me not to leave her when we felt this amazing together. "I'm not walking away from this—from you."

3

TITAN

THE MORE TIMES I slept with Hunt, the better it got.

He was a king in bed, having everything that I craved in a partner. He was confident, beautiful, and drop-dead sexy.

I didn't know what I loved more—his kiss or cock.

I loved it all.

We returned to New York and got back to work. Taking a week off pushed me back, so I had to play catch-up to stay on top of my empire. I didn't contact Hunt for several days because I was too busy.

He didn't contact me either—probably for the exact same reason.

Thorn texted me. *I'm gonna stop by in ten minutes— unless you've got company.*

I'm alone.

Then I'll see you soon.

Thorn rode the elevator to my floor, having the key code to my penthouse so I didn't have to buzz him up every time. He walked into the living room in jeans and a gray t-shirt, looking handsome but casual in his street clothes. Most of the time I saw him he was in a suit, something specifically tailored to his tall height and broad shoulders. He walked inside with dazzling eyes and greeted me with a smile. "How's it going, Old Fashion?"

"Good. I've been busy since I came back from Italy." I poured him a glass of his favorite wine and made myself my drink. We took a seat at the dining table, the Manhattan lights in the background.

He took a long drink, devouring it like water instead of alcohol. "How was that?"

"Pretty good."

"Did you and your boy toy have a good time?"

"Actually, we did. Would have been more fun if his brother hadn't been around."

"Cockblocks...hate 'em. How's Diesel Hunt working out for you?" He asked me about all my relationships, so this wasn't unusual.

"He's everything I hoped for—and more."

A quiet smile stretched his lips. "Seems like a guy with the whole package."

"Yes. And he definitely *has* the whole package."

He winked. "Dirty girl."

"Just a woman who knows what she wants." I remembered what Hunt had told me about Thorn, that Thorn had mentioned our relationship to him in passing. "Hunt said you spoke to him about me at the charity gala...encouraged him to pursue me."

"I did." He swirled the wine in his glass. "And it looks like my advice worked."

"Why would you say anything to him at all? I didn't know if he was trustworthy."

"He's a straight shooter," he said dismissively. "I can tell. Besides, friends help each other get laid. That's the foundation of any friendship."

"Well, I can get laid without your help."

He winked again. "Because you're a dirty girl."

I rolled my eyes and held back my chuckle. Only Thorn could joke with me like that and get away with it.

"I'm glad things worked out. Looks like you two found a compromise."

I loved our current arrangement. But I wasn't sure how much I would love the second half of it. "Yes...six weeks for me. Six weeks for him."

Thorn set his glass down and ignored it. "You think you can handle it?"

"Looks like I'm going to have to," I said. "And he

didn't give me much of a choice. It was either this or not have him at all."

"You must really like the guy."

"I do..." I loved everything about him. He was so much more than the businessman I read about. He had an edge as sharp as the blade of a sword, but he was as gentle as soft cotton at the same time. He knew how to fuck hard—and how to fuck slow. He made my mouth tremble every time he kissed me, and when we weren't screwing, he spoke to me like a friend. He looked at me as an equal, always respecting everything I had to say. I couldn't count the number of times men talked over me like my voice didn't matter, like they knew more than me before they even gave me a chance to speak. My conversations with Hunt were never like that. "How was your trip to Chicago?"

"Just a lot of working, drinking, and fucking."

"Was the fucking good?"

He shrugged. "Good enough. But I got a lot of work done. That was what I cared about the most."

"Good for you."

"My parents are coming into town tomorrow. I told them we would have dinner together."

"And you didn't think I had plans?"

He smiled. "I knew you would reschedule them for me. You love my mom."

"Because she's sweet. Not sure how you didn't inherit that trait."

He rolled his eyes at the taunt. "Real men aren't sweet. Women wouldn't like it if we were."

"True."

"We're eating at The Jewel. My assistant already made reservations. I'll pick you up at seven."

"Sounds good to me. I love their food."

"How was the fashion show? Were you bored out of your mind?"

Hunt was there, so I was never bored. "No. But Connor tried to rekindle our fire a bit."

"I can't blame him." Thorn had the brightest blue eyes I'd ever seen. That was one of the reasons he had so many admirers. They were bluer than every untouched ocean in the world. "Realizes what he lost. But that ship has sailed, right?"

"Yep." Now my ship was anchored in Hunt's harbor.

"Diesel doesn't like me." Thorn looked at me as he waited for me to confirm this piece of information.

"No. He's just jealous."

"Did you tell him there's nothing to be jealous of?"

"Many times."

"And?"

"He doesn't understand our relationship, and that frustrates him."

"He doesn't need to know. He wouldn't understand anyway."

I wasn't sure. Hunt seemed to be a reasonable guy. He understood how the world worked just as well as I did. If I explained my situation with Thorn, Hunt would probably understand it completely. "I think he would get it, but he still doesn't need to know."

"How's Pilar?"

"Good. Just landed the cover of a sports magazine."

"Not surprised," he said. "She's too exceptional to be anywhere else."

I finished my glass and cut myself off. I'd already had too many drinks today. "Would you like to join me for dinner? I was just about to throw something together."

"I'd love to—if Hunt isn't coming by."

"That won't be until later. We don't eat together."

He grinned. "Just fucking?"

"Yep."

"I like the way you run things, Titan. Just like a business."

"My life is much simpler that way." I walked into the kitchen and grabbed everything out of the fridge.

Thorn fell into sync with me, washing the broccolini before slicing it into perfect strips.

I handled the chicken and carrots.

"I think you should move in on Bruce Carol this week. His stock is about to drop."

I'd been so busy this last week I hadn't really thought about it. "You're right."

"I'd offer to take care of it, but I'm sure you can handle this one. Bruce and I have never gotten along."

"And you think he'll get along with your girlfriend?"

Thorn set the vegetables aside before he grabbed a pan and set it on the stove. "When she's as beautiful as you, yes."

I grinned and kept my eyes focused on what I was doing. "You don't have to suck up to me, Thorn. You already got me."

"I wasn't." He nudged me in the side gently. "I meant it."

I WALKED INTO BRUCE'S BUILDING, CHECKED IN WITH HIS assistant, and then waited in the lobby. I wore a black pencil skirt with a fitted blue blouse, going for traditional colors that weren't too bold. I left my hair down, letting it curl around my shoulders. I wore my favorite pair of black heels, even though Bruce Carol would have no idea what brand they were or how much they cost.

I waited ten minutes before I was finally called into

the conference room. "Mr. Carol, how are you?" I walked up to him with my hand extended, a smile on my face.

Bruce was in his late fifties, packing on weight throughout the decades and with a face covered with hair. He wore large glasses he'd obviously kept since the eighties. Despite the way one of his biggest investments was going under, he was a respectable businessman who had accomplished a lot in the last thirty years. "Good." He shook my hand, not mirroring my same smile. "Thanks for coming by." He sat down at the seat at the head of the table, and he didn't offer me anything to drink. His hands came together on the desk, and he looked at the time on his watch.

That wasn't a good start.

I opened my folder and got right to the point. "I understand your investment in your company, while a great concept, isn't doing well. Every quarter, your profits have steadily declined. In the last quarter, you're actually down by fifty percent. This isn't public knowledge just yet, and I'd like to put an offer on the table. I can assure you I'll give you more than a fair deal, and everything will be wrapped up before the media gets to blast it on the front page of every single newspaper. We can simply say the company has been taken over by Titan Industries."

"Looks like you're jumping ahead before you've even

made an offer." He tapped his fingers against the desk, his chubby fingers echoing quietly in the room.

He was an asshole with wounded pride. I should have known he wouldn't take this well.

"I'm not sure how you've figured all of this out, so I must have traitors in the company."

Or Thorn and I were smarter than he gave us credit for. "Money always leaves a trail." I pulled out the offer letter and slid it across the table toward him. "This is what I'm willing to offer you. There are a few stipulations, but nothing major."

He looked it over, his eyes quickly scanning the words. "No."

I waited patiently for an elaboration.

But it never came.

"The floor is open for negotiation."

He pushed the paper back toward me. "Double your offer, and we have a deal."

As an attempt to control the situation, it was pathetic. He had no tact whatsoever. I was transparent in my meetings, getting right to the point to save time. But I also thought of every move before I made it. Bruce obviously didn't. No wonder why his company was going under. "No." I crossed out the initial offer I'd made and gave him a ten percent increase before I pushed it back toward him. "This is my final offer. Anyone else who comes through that door isn't going to offer you anything near this. Consider yourself lucky it's on the table at all."

He stared at the number for a long time before he turned it over. "I have another offer coming in this afternoon. I'll wait to hear that one first."

Another offer? Who else knew about Bruce's failing holdings? I couldn't allow myself to look surprised, whether he was bluffing or not. I had to keep my cool, act like I didn't want this company as much as I did.

"But I'll think about your offer, sweetheart."

Sweetheart. I hated being called that. If I were a man, he wouldn't call me "sport" or "champ." It was insulting, belittling me.

But I acted like it had no effect on me. "I'll be in touch to follow up soon." I rose from my seat and was only mildly offended when he didn't rise as well. I didn't receive a handshake or even a second glance from him.

I walked out, knowing he was staring at my ass the whole way. He didn't give me the respect of looking me in the eye, but he had no problem staring at my behind. I knew he was looking when I spotted his reflection in the glass door.

Asshole.

I walked back to the lobby, holding back the annoyance that must be obvious on my face. I heard the assistant's voice trail to me as I approached the lobby. "Mr. Hunt, Mr. Carol will see you now."

I nearly stopped in my tracks when I heard that name.

I rounded the corner and reached the lobby just when he stood up, buttoning the front of his suit as he moved. He carried a satchel over his shoulder, his computer no doubt stuffed inside. His face was cleanly shaven, and he looked even more handsome than the last time I saw him. His shiny watch was on his wrist, and he wore shiny dress shoes.

It took him a moment to notice me, and when he did, he didn't give the slightest reaction. It wasn't clear if he already knew I would be there, or he was just a professional at hiding his thoughts.

I didn't know.

We walked past each other, time slowing down as we came into close proximity. The look he gave me was the kind I'd never seen before. It was like he didn't know me at all. His lethal professionalism was at the forefront of his mind. He must have known exactly why I was there. If he didn't know when he walked into the building, he knew now.

"Titan." His masculine voice brushed over my skin like sandpaper against rocks. It didn't contain the affection I was used to receiving from him. We were both after the same thing, a company that could be worth billions someday. Just because we were sleeping together, it didn't change the fact that we were competitors—and we were ruthless.

"Hunt." I walked past him, giving him the same look of indifference he gave me. The smell of his cologne still lingered in my nose even though our proximity had ended. Maybe I thought I smelled him when I didn't. Just like how I pictured his hands on my body even though we were no longer near each other.

I made it out of the building, and the unease about my meeting with Bruce Carol caught up with me. It didn't go well, and I hadn't realized I had a top-notch competitor working against me. Hunt brought the same resources to the table, and he could make an offer just as good as mine.

I was about to lose this deal—and there was nothing I could do about it.

THORN'S MOTHER KISSED EACH OF MY CHEEKS BEFORE SHE hugged me, embracing me like she was my mother. "It was so nice seeing you, Tatum. You make my son into a fine man."

"Thank you, Liv. But he was already a fine man before I came along."

His father kissed my cheek next before he hugged his son. "Thanks for dinner."

"No problem, Dad." Thorn patted him on the back before he stepped back. "Have fun in Bora Bora. Take lots of pictures."

"We will." Liv gave a wave before they got into the backseat of their car. The windows were tinted, but I suspected they were waving at us anyway. The driver pulled away and took them back into Manhattan traffic.

"I was a fine man before you came along?" Thorn asked with a laugh. "Even my parents don't believe that." He pulled out his phone and texted his driver, telling him to pick us up in front of the restaurant.

"What was I supposed to say?" I asked incredulously. "That you're the biggest shithead in the world?"

He grinned at the insult. "At least you'd be honest."

"I'm not gonna insult a mother by saying that about her son."

"Why?" he asked. "It's not like she doesn't know. She raised me, you know." He spotted the car as it pulled up to the curb. He opened the back door and helped me inside before he scooted to the seat beside me. Once we were alone in a car with tinted windows, we broke apart, and I sat next to the window. I was wearing a long cocktail dress that was fit for a ball. Thorn wore a black suit that complemented me.

The second we were alone, it was back to business. "How'd it go with Bruce?"

I'd failed to mention this to him, knowing he would take the news as hard as I did. "Pretty terrible, honestly."

He brushed it off. "You just think it went terrible. You're the best in the business, Titan. Don't underestimate yourself. I would have gone myself if I didn't think you could handle it."

I appreciated the praise, but that wouldn't console me this time. "The second I walked in there, he was cold. He barely listened to me, make ridiculous demands, and then didn't even walk me to the door—but had no problem staring at my ass."

"In his defense, you have a very nice ass."

I rolled my eyes.

"Come on, you know all men are dogs. It's never bothered you before, so don't let it bother you now."

"I already knew the meeting was going poorly before we even said two words to each other. But when I reached the lobby, I knew exactly why he was behaving that way. There was another offer on the table, and he knew he was going to take it before he even met with me."

Thorn turned my way, the features of his face falling

into seriousness. His blue eyes didn't look quite as beautiful as they usually did. Now they looked like blue ice. "Another offer? Who else knows about this?"

I shouldn't have underestimated the man I was screwing. I was powerfully attracted to him for a reason, because he was a ruthless tyrant who intended to own the entire city someday—if not the world. "Diesel Hunt."

Thorn's eyes narrowed in obvious rage. "Did you tell him?"

"No. I never mentioned a single thing to him."

"Did he go through your things?"

"I never have my laptop around when he's at my place, and we're always in the same room together. Besides, I don't think he would do something like that. He's far too respectable."

"When it comes to business, no one is a saint."

"I think he figured it out from his own sources."

"Did he seem surprised to see you?"

"No. But neither did I."

Thorn sighed and looked out the window, falling into suffocating silence. "Titan, we can't lose this deal."

"I know."

"It's an opportunity of a lifetime."

"Whatever Hunt offers, you have to match it."

"I'm not sure if the offers are up for debate. I'll call

Bruce tomorrow and feel him out." I was embarrassed that I lost to Hunt without even knowing what happened. I just assumed he won because of the way Bruce behaved. I had the confidence to never give up, but I also had the intuition to know when it was a losing battle. It was obvious that Bruce preferred Hunt before he even met with me.

A part of me couldn't blame him. Hunt was an intellect with a knack for business. He was one of the most fascinating people in the world for a reason. I was disappointed Hunt would get this business, but at the same time, I thought he deserved it.

Because I respected him so damn much.

But Thorn didn't feel the same way. He kept looking out the window, his annoyance filling the air like humidity. "You guys should have some kind of boundaries for this sort of thing."

"I told him we wouldn't mix business with pleasure —and we're abiding by that promise. It would be naïve of me to expect him to back off just for me. It's not like I would back off for him. He wouldn't respect me if I did, and I wouldn't respect him either."

Thorn growled before he turned back to me. "Well, the fight isn't over. Talk to Bruce tomorrow, and we'll go from there."

I looked out the window when the conversation was

over, feeling Thorn's overwhelming disappointment in the turn of events. Thorn was an excellent partner because he was transparent. It was never a challenge to figure out what he was thinking, and if I was ever unsure, all I had to do was ask. He amplified my confidence with his praise, and he helped me overcome my weaknesses. And when he was disappointed, like he was now, he didn't hide it.

4

HUNT

I WASN'T EXPECTING to see Titan when I walked into Bruce's office.

But I shouldn't have been surprised.

It was naïve to think I was the only one who knew Bruce was going under. If someone else was going to figure it out, it was going to be Titan. She strutted into that office and worked her magic.

I had to step it up.

Just because I was screwing her didn't mean I would bow out. I was a gentleman—but only so much. That company was going to be mine, and I was willing to undercut her as much as possible to make that happen.

When I met with Bruce, I made an offer he couldn't refuse. A five percent stake in the company, including the buyout.

After wanting to buy her publishing house, I learned

a lot about Titan. She ran her businesses in very specific ways. She would never make an offer like that, no matter how much money was on the table. She was the exclusive owner of everything she slapped her name on. Giving a cut like this was something she was too proud to do.

So I did it.

All was fair in love and war, right?

Bruce didn't hide his smile when he accepted my offer. We shook hands—and the rest was history.

I hadn't spoken to Titan since, and I wondered how this would affect our relationship. She said business was a conflict of interest and we should never speak about it, so it shouldn't have any hold over us at all.

But who knows. I knew she wanted this company as much as I did. She might be too resentful.

I was about to find out.

She texted me later that evening. It'd been seven days since we'd last gotten together. I'd been too busy at work to see her, and she must have been just as swamped. But now I was craving that body, and there wasn't a doubt in my mind she was craving mine. *Come over.*

I loved reading her messages, loved how simple they were. I didn't need to read between the lines to figure out what her mood was. She said exactly what was on her mind, leaving little to the imagination. *Be there in ten minutes.*

I used the key code she gave me and rode the elevator right into her living room. The doors opened to the sound of classical music playing softly in the background. On the coffee table was a tray with a bucket of ice, a bottle of whiskey, and two glasses. But the woman I wanted was nowhere in sight.

She appeared down the hallway, wearing black lingerie and sky-high heels. She walked in them like she was barefoot, having complete control over the way her body glided. She locked eyes with me and walked right up to me, her confidence as forceful as ever.

I'd missed this.

Her body was perfect. Fair skin against dark lace. Her eyelashes were thick with jet-black mascara, contrasting against the green color of her sparkling eyes. She wore bright red lipstick, making her look sultry and erotic. I loved the way she owned the room, making everything bow down to her—including me.

She walked up to me and slid her hands up my chest, her face close to mine. It didn't seem like she knew Bruce had picked my offer. If she had, something would be different. But everything was exactly the same. She pressed a gentle kiss to the corner of my mouth, taking in a soft breath when she felt my flesh against hers.

My cock started to throb.

She pulled away and met my gaze. "Congratulations on your deal." Her hands slowly began to unbutton my collared shirt. "I know we don't talk about business, but I wanted you to know that." She moved until she undid the very last button, her eyes on me as her fingers worked.

She took her loss with elegance, making her even classier than before. I respected her for losing so gracefully, for being so logical that it didn't affect her attraction to me. She wasn't the kind of businesswoman who was used to losing. She always got what she wanted. But she held her head high, making her look like the victor even though I was the one who'd acquired the business. "Thank you."

"You deserve it." She pushed the shirt over my shoulders until it fell on the floor.

Fuck, now I wanted her more.

Her hands went to my jeans, and she got them loose. She didn't ask what I offered Bruce. She didn't ask how I knew his business was failing. She didn't ask anything, knowing there was nothing more to say on the matter.

It was time to move on.

She pushed my pants to my ankles then stood in

front of me again. When she wore heels like that, it was easier for her to kiss me. She tilted her chin up and put her mouth on mine, transferring her heat into my body.

I kissed her back, no longer thinking about my most recent business conquest. Now I was just thinking about this unbelievable woman standing in front of me, my competitor and my lover.

Her hand wrapped around my pulsing cock, and she gently massaged it, her ministrations increasing in intensity the longer she kissed me. She rubbed my cock the way I touched myself when I was alone in my penthouse. She touched me exactly the way I wanted to be touched—because she knew me so well. She played out my fantasies, knowing what they were before I even did.

Her fingers moved to my balls, and she cupped them gently before she massaged them with her slender fingertips. She played with my dick so eloquently, gripping him hard then gently massaging him.

All the while she was kissing me.

She sucked my bottom lip into her mouth before her tongue circled mine. Her kiss was never the same. Sometimes she was harsh, and sometimes she was soft. Right now, she was somewhere in between.

My hand moved into her hair, and I deepened the kiss, suppressing the moan that was sitting in the back of my throat. My other hand gripped her hip, my fingers kneading her bare ass.

She kept stroking my length, her fingers smearing my lubrication over the rest of my dick.

I already wanted to come.

I wouldn't be surprised if she were doing this on purpose, bringing me to the edge just to make me wait. It was torture, but my climaxes were ten times more powerful.

She broke our kiss and stared at my lips. Her hands gripped my base, but she stopped stroking me. "Take off your shoes and sit on the couch." She walked into the living room, her ass unbelievably perky in her black thong. She had long and slender legs, small muscles connecting together to form perfectly chiseled limbs. She grabbed the bottle of whiskey and took a drink.

With my eyes trained on her, I followed her directions. There was a plastic sheet over the couch and along the floor. I sat directly on it and wondered what kind of plans she had. Whatever they were, it involved something messy.

And I looked forward to it.

She held up a black scarf, something from her wardrobe, and then walked around the couch before she secured it around my head. She blindfolded me, taking away my sight and enhancing my sense of sound.

Her footsteps echoed on the hardwood floor as she came back to the front. "Don't move." She gripped both of my wrists and pushed them into the cushions on either side of me. I heard the sound of the bottle as she lifted it from the table. An instant later, liquid splashed on my chest.

She poured liquor all over me, letting it run down my body until it soaked into my dick. I heard her position herself on her knees on the floor then lean over me, her soft body coming into contact with mine.

She kissed my chest, licking away the whiskey. She dragged her tongue across my skin, soaking up every drop before she slowly migrated to my stomach. Rivers of whiskey had formed between my abs, and she sucked it up with her pursed lips. "Diesel Hunt, you have the sexiest body..."

My hands formed fists on either side of my body. I squeezed tightly, stretching my knuckles. A compliment like that didn't escape Titan's mouth often. I was one of the few who actually got to hear it. Now I wanted to plant her right on my dick and fuck her pussy the way she was fucking me with her mouth.

But I couldn't move.

She drifted down my body until she reached my soaked cock as it lay against my stomach. She licked from the base to the tip, drinking up all the whiskey that had pooled there. When she didn't get enough, she put her dick in her mouth and sucked every drop away.

Fuck.

Now I wanted to grab her even more. I wanted to yank this blindfold off my face so I could watch her eat me. My hands shook beside me, and I was doing my best to keep them in place even though they desperately wanted to move.

She moved farther down and drew my balls into her mouth, licking away the whiskey that had absorbed into the skin. She was devouring all of me, going over each section with purposeful slowness.

This woman was killing me.

I wanted to drink an entire bottle of whiskey off her body.

She ran her hands up my muscular thighs, squeezing the muscles before she moved down again. I heard the sucking noises her mouth made when she pulled my skin into her mouth. She became more aggressive, devouring me completely.

"Titan, fuck me." She was calling the shots, and I was supposed to sit back and take it. But I was tired of waiting, so sexually frustrated I was about to explode.

"I'll fuck you when I'm ready."

My hands formed fists again, and my chest rose and fell deeply. I continued to take in breath, but I wasn't getting enough air. I was losing my restraint, being tested in a way I'd never been tested before.

She sucked my dick longer, pouring more whiskey onto my skin before licking it away. She took my big cock into her mouth without choking, using her small tongue to massage every groove of my hard length.

I wanted to come, but I was more anxious to fuck her.

To feel her pussy.

She finally finished torturing me and straddled my hips. She pointed my cock at her entrance and slowly slid down, taking in every single inch of my cock with purposeful slowness.

Thank fucking god.

She gripped my shoulders for balance and bounced on my dick, moving with our mutual slickness. She was soaked, and I was making her even more soaked. Without thinking twice about it, my hands moved to her ass, and I guided her up and down, grunting because she felt so good.

"Hands." She slapped me across the face, a light tap that barely tingled my nerves.

Instead of putting my hands back where they belonged, I kept them in place. I gripped her harder and moved her up and down my length again, taking her with deep thrusts.

She slapped me again, this time harder.

I'd never been slapped by a woman, but damn, I liked it. I loved the way her small palm collided with my face, exerting so much power with a simple touch. I loved the ferocity of the smack, the way she exerted her control.

I pulled my blindfold off next, wanting to see the fire in her eyes.

She was pissed—but aroused.

She didn't stop riding my length, continuing at a deep and steady pace. She took in my length over and over, sitting wearing the top part of her lingerie. Her tits were pushed up together in a black push-up bra, her cleavage sexy. "Hunt."

"I want to look at you." I thrust from underneath, watching her chest flush in desire.

She slapped me again, this time hard.

I turned with the hit, enjoying every second of that flushed heat. My skin fired off with irritated nerve endings, but I liked the pain.

I loved the pain.

"Hands off," she commanded. "And mask back on."

"No." Her pussy was getting tighter, and she was getting wetter. She liked my obedience, but she liked my disobedience even more. She told me to obey, but it was obvious she didn't really want me to.

Her eyes flashed even brighter. She hit me again, putting all of her momentum into it.

My face turned with the hit, and heat flushed through my body. I loved it. I loved being smacked by this woman. "Fuck, you're the sexiest damn thing in the world." I rolled her to her back on the couch, keeping my dick firmly inside her, and then I fucked her so hard into the couch I almost broke it.

The second I was in control, she yielded. She hooked her arms around my shoulders and dug her nails into my skin. One leg was pinned against the back of the couch, while the other knee was against her chest.

I conquered her, fucking her into the couch and giving her as much of my cock as she could handle. I pounded into her harder than I ever had before, more aroused than I'd ever been in my life. We both smelled of whiskey and sweat, the alcohol rubbing into each other's skin. It stained her lingerie and seeped into her hair. She was supposed to be in charge, but I couldn't hold back this time. I hadn't fucked her in so long, and I missed her.

I missed her so damn much.

Titan screamed when I made her come, her yells echoing inside the penthouse. Her pussy became so tight it nearly bruised my dick. She clenched around me like an anaconda squeezed its prey. She panted against my mouth, breathing deeply once the climax started to drift away.

Without waiting for permission, I exploded. I shoved my dick deep inside her and dumped my come inside her soaked pussy. I gave her everything I had, moaning and groaning because it felt so incredible. Every time I was inside her, it was even better than my last experience. But tonight, her channel felt more spectacular than before. Probably because I hadn't had it in so long.

Jesus, she was heaven.

I stayed on top of her when I was finished, my softening cock still deep inside her. My forehead rested against hers, and I closed my eyes, feeling my cheek burn from the way she slapped me so many times.

But a burn had never felt so good.

Her nails retracted, and she skimmed her fingertips down my back, touching me softly after the way she'd gripped me so fiercely.

I opened my eyes and looked at her, seeing the soft expression she wore when I first came inside.

"I'll let that one go since it's been so long since we've seen each other. But not again." Even though she was pinned underneath me, half my body size, she exerted a shadow of power that rivaled my own. She commanded the situation with little effort.

It validated my existing obsession. "Yes, Boss Lady."

SHE SIPPED HER GLASS OF WATER AND STARED AT THE TV. The sound was on mute, and there was a replay of a baseball game that aired earlier that day. She wore my white collared shirt with just her panties underneath. Her hair was untidy and her makeup smeared, but she looked stunning that way.

Because I was the cause of the disarray.

I drank my glass as I watched her, clean from rinsing off in her shower. Now I sat in my boxers on the couch, the plastic cover gone. I watched her, intrigued by this mysterious woman and wondering what her thoughts were.

She always had a glass of water after sex. And she always had a fresh vase of flowers on most surfaces. I'd never seen wilting flowers anywhere near her. She must change them out every two days, like clockwork. She was constantly dressed in dark colors, but she surrounded herself with stark femininity. She turned to me and set her glass down. "Are you hungry?"

She'd never offered me food before. "A little."

"I have some leftovers from last night. Would you like some?"

"Did you make it?"

"Yes."

"Then yes." I wanted to taste her cooking—since I'd tasted everything else of hers.

She walked into the kitchen, heated up two plates of food, and then returned. She made leftover chicken breast, plain with salt and paper and lemon marinade, along with broccoli and asparagus.

The meat was tender enough to cut into with a fork, and I ate while I watched her on the other couch.

She took small bites, taking a long time to chew her food before she swallowed it.

It didn't surprise me that this was the kind of diet she had. A woman didn't have legs like that without watching every little thing she ate. She drank so much she had to offset it in some way. She obviously cared more about liquor than food.

"This is good," I said between bites. "Thank you."

"You're welcome." She finished everything before she set the empty plate on the table.

I put mine down too and watched her, wondering if she wanted me to leave or not. I had no reason to stay, but it was hard for me to get up. Whenever I was with her, I was comfortable. I didn't think about work or the other bullshit in my life. I didn't think about anything, actually. It was nice. "How did you know about Bruce Carol?"

She crossed her legs and turned her head in my direction. "We don't talk about business."

"The deal has been done. I don't see the harm."

"I do." She grabbed her water again.

I should have known that would be her reaction. She wasn't intimidated by my success, knowing it was no reflection on her own accomplishments. She was confident enough not to let my victory interfere with our relationship, but she wasn't going to change her mind about her initial rules.

I remembered the night we sat together in her hotel room. We were both satisfied after an intense round of fucking, so we sat in the dark and talked—and drank. I learned she was a writer, that she had a sweet smile when she was comfortable enough to show it.

I liked that conversation as much as the sex.

But I couldn't ask her anything deep directly. I had to circle in slowly. Otherwise, she'd throw her walls up. "How long have you been living here?"

"I bought this place five years ago. Before that, I was on Madison."

"It's nice."

"Thanks. Your place is nice too."

"Thanks." They were similar, probably equal in value. We both had the same view of the city, on the same floor. I was just closer to my office, and she was closer to hers. "Where else do you have real estate?"

"Rhode Island," she answered. "It's a beach house. I go there to unwind, to have celebrations."

"Nice."

"I also have places in San Diego and Aspen. What about you?"

Now the dialogue was open. We weren't talking about anything important, but the conversation was nice anyway. I enjoyed getting to know her, having a relationship with her besides sex. She had a group of friends that had access to all of her secrets, so she was willing to share her life with people—if she trusted you. "I have places everywhere. One in Malibu, Hawaii, Lake Como, Cannes...the list goes on."

"You love the south of France?" she asked.

"It's beautiful. You?"

"There's no place like it. I've never purchased anything there because I love staying at the resorts. Sometimes it's nice to have your kitchen and your own space, and other times, I'm in the mood for someone to cater to my every need."

I nodded in understanding. "Do you have a yacht?"

"Yes, in San Diego."

She liked her toys as much as I did. "I'd love to see it sometime—if we're ever there at the same time."

"Maybe," she said noncommittally.

I tried to keep the conversation going. "I bought a small plane a few years ago. I have my pilot's license, and I take it for a drive sometimes. Or I should say, I take it for a flight sometimes."

She turned my way, her interest piqued. "Yeah?"

I nodded.

"I've always wanted to fly."

"You should. Nothing like it."

"I just never have the time... I guess I'll have to make the time."

When I glanced at the clock, I saw that it was nearly ten. It was time for me to head home and get ready for my day tomorrow, but I continued to stay.

Wasn't sure why.

"Have you seen the footage of the commercial yet?" she asked.

"No." I hadn't spoken to my brother since we came back to the city. "I'm sure it came out great, though." Titan would steal the show with those flirtatious eyes and beautiful smile.

"You have another brother?" she asked.

"Yes. A younger one." She said she wouldn't ask personal questions, but maybe this didn't fall into that category because she'd already met Brett.

"What does he do?"

"Lives in Manhattan. He's still working for my father's company. The place is his when my dad croaks."

Titan's green eyes concentrated on my face, her intelligent brain working behind her eyes. She examined me in silence, considering how she would approach the situation. She never asked about my father, but she obviously knew we had bad blood. She must have figured that out when she Googled me, just how I figured things out when I Googled her. "You aren't close, then?"

"We don't talk." I hadn't spoken to him in years. When Dad and I went our separate ways, Jax followed our father. Instead of branching on his own and making his own fortune, he chose to stick it out and inherit everything my father built in his lifetime.

Pussy shit.

When Titan knew she was in dangerous territory, she stopped asking questions.

It made me realize I wanted to know more about her, but I wasn't willing to give up anything in return. Wasn't exactly fair.

"Were you close with your parents?" I wasn't going to pretend I didn't already have access to this basic information. I knew they were both gone.

To my surprise, she answered the question. "I don't remember my mother. She took off when I was young, maybe five or six."

Took off? I'd assumed she passed away. "She left you?"

Titan didn't seem upset about this aspect of her life because she remained as unmoved as ever. "My father didn't talk about it much. He just said she couldn't handle being a mother and left. Apparently, she slipped out in the middle of the night and left a note. I found the note when I was going through my father's things. But I never read it."

How did she have the strength to ignore it?

She answered my unspoken question. "My father still spoke highly of her as time went on. Even after she left both of us, he still loved her. I never understood it. Since he didn't want me to hate her, I chose not to read it. He wouldn't have wanted me to."

"Then you were close with him?"

A painful smile crept onto her features, her eyes reflective of the memories she still held in her heart. "My father was my best friend. I still miss him —every day."

Seeing the combination of her emotions, the happiness she felt from loving him and the devastation she felt now that he was gone, burned into my skin in a way I hadn't felt before. I pitied her, wanted to make her feel better. Now I wished I hadn't mentioned anything at all so she wouldn't have had to experience this pain right now. "I'm sorry."

After a deep sigh, she controlled her thoughts and pulled herself out of the dive, returning to the rigid woman who worked her stilettos every day. "But that's how life goes. We live and we die. My fate won't be any different."

Neither would mine.

She rose from the couch and collected the plates. "You should get going, Hunt. I have a long day tomorrow." She walked into the kitchen and turned on the faucet, doing the dishes. I pulled on my clothes, thinking about everything she'd just shared with me. When I approached her in the right way, she opened like the petals of a flower on a warm spring day. Her heart was open, and her thoughts were no longer invisible. She was just a woman—not a ruler. I felt special that she'd shared that with me, told me something she probably didn't say to anyone else.

I walked into the kitchen and saw her standing there in my shirt. It was all I was missing, but that wasn't why I walked inside. I came up behind her and pressed my chest to her back. She stiffened at my touch, immediately feeling my powerful physique against her. I turned off the water and wrapped my arms around her, hugging her to me.

I held her like that for a long time, my intentions unknown. I didn't want sex from her. I didn't want anything from her.

I just wanted to be there for her.

Her arms moved over mine, and she rested the back of her head against my chest. She didn't push me off and encourage me to leave. She let me support her, let me be her crutch. She allowed another layer to come off, to let me witness an even softer side of her.

My lips moved against her hair, and I pressed a kiss to her hairline.

Her chest immediately rose at the contact, her body automatically taking a breath.

She felt something.

It was undeniable.

And I felt something too.

I SAT AT MY DESK AND FLIPPED THROUGH THE NEWS ON my phone.

The third story down was an article about Titan.

And Thorn.

THORN CUTLER AND TATUM TITAN SPEND A QUIET

evening out to dinner with the Cutler family. Proposal coming soon?

THERE WAS A PICTURE OF THE FOUR OF THEM HAVING dinner, laughing as they shared a bottle of wine. Thorn's arm was draped over the back of Titan's chair, showing minor affection, but enough to annoy me.

Piss me off, actually.

I shouldn't care.

Fuck, I don't care.

But goddammit, I do care.

Natalie's voice came through the intercom. "The team is ready to head to Bruce Carol's office, sir."

Her voice disrupted my thoughts, but not enough to sway my anger. "I'll be there in five minutes." I had nothing to finish up, no phone call to make. I just needed to sit there for a moment, to let the rage slowly leave my body with every pump of my heart. With every beat, it dissolved the annoyance in my bloodstream and cleaned it out.

The pulse in my temple was loud, and my cheek started to hurt because I was tensing my jaw so tightly.

My reaction was stupid. Titan told me about her relationship with Thorn. She wasn't sleeping with him.

Thorn confirmed the same thing, even encouraging us to work out our differences and be together.

So I shouldn't care.

But something about their arrangement bothered me—probably because I was left in the dark. What was their connection? What did they mean to each other? What did each one get out of this lie?

And why the fuck wouldn't she tell me?

I was fucking her. I had a right to know.

Natalie's voice came through the intercom again. "Sir, it's been ten minutes. Just wanted to see if I could help you with anything."

I needed to bottle these thoughts inside and forget about them. "I'm coming."

I WALKED INTO THE BOARDROOM WITH MY LEGAL TEAM. Bruce was sitting on one side of the table, his lawyers flanking him on either side. They were all middle-aged men with collars that fit too tightly around the necks. Stubby fingers with wedding rings and knuckle hair were marked on all of them. "Afternoon, gentlemen." I walked to each one and shook hands. Bruce stood up to greet me, giving me a smile before patting me on the back.

"It's great to see you, Mr. Hunt. Let's get down to business, shall we?"

"Right to the point, Bruce," I said. "I like it." I moved back to my side of the table and handed out the contracts. We were officially signing the paperwork and wiring the money for ownership of the company. It was something I couldn't delegate to someone else to do since I was the one acquiring it. But I'd rather have spent my time focusing on my next venture. "As you can see, I've agreed to accept all of your requests. Your stake in the company will be paid quarterly."

Bruce flipped through the contract, unsurprised by what he saw. His legal team looked through it more carefully, making sure it matched the one my assistant had emailed a few days prior.

I sat back in my chair and watched Bruce, never taking my eyes off him. Until the company was officially mine, I still had something to lose. I had to remain as poised as ever, examining my surroundings for any sign of disaster.

"Everything looks in order to me," Bruce said. "You've given me more than a fair offer, Hunt. Much better than what that tight-ass offered me."

My fingers rested on the table, and they immediately retracted, forming a fist. I was jumping to a conclusion when I assumed he was referring to Titan, but she was the only other person who made him an offer that I knew of. "Excuse me?"

"Tatum Titan," he said. "I'm sure you know she met me with me first."

I stared at him down, my eyes so concentrated they started to water. I couldn't blink to give them a respite from the air. Now I stared at Bruce with adrenaline pumping through my heart, offended as if he'd just insulted me to my face.

"Her offer was piss," he said. "And even if it weren't, I'd rather lose the company than hand it over to a woman. Maybe if she offered to suck my dick, I would have played a different tune." He laughed uproariously like it was the funniest thing he'd ever heard. A few of his lawyers chuckled, probably because they were excited they were about to be paid. "But she does have a nice nectarine, so I'll give her that."

My knuckles turned white.

Thankfully, there were six feet in between us. Any less than that, and I may have grabbed his scalp and slammed his face into the table. I dragged my hand across my face, trying to control my clenched jaw and flaring temper.

The lawyers were near the end of the contact, almost ready to cross the T's and dot the I's.

Instead of thinking about the fortune I was about to

attain, I kept picturing a pool of blood surrounding his dead body. As if he'd just insulted my dead mother, I was livid. He crossed a line I hadn't realized existed. He provoked me in a way that made smoke come out of my ears.

I despised this man with every fiber of my being.

I rose to my feet, everyone shifting their gazes to watch what I was doing. I buttoned the front of my suit, staring down the man I'd immediately marked as my enemy. "Deal's off. Let's go."

My team looked at me, confusion written all over their faces. But they didn't dare question me in front of anyone. They closed their portfolios and their laptops and packed up.

Bruce's confusion was ten times as strong than everyone else's. "Mr. Hunt, what's going on?"

"Deal's off." Just because I spoke calmly didn't mean my rage was under control. My ferocity filled up every corner of the room. People became smaller as I doubled in size. "My offer is officially withdrawn. I won't be doing business with you—and I'll never do business with you." I turned around and walked to the door just as Natalie opened it for me.

"Hunt, what the hell?" Bruce stood up, both of his hands hitting the surface of the table. "We had a deal. You can't just walk out of here like this."

I turned around, and when he saw my gaze, he shrank back slightly. "I don't do business with assholes. And I can do whatever the hell I want, Bruce. I'm one of the richest men in the world, and now, you're one of the poorest."

5

TITAN

THORN CALLED me while I was at work. He usually only contacted me outside of working hours because he was too busy handling his own businesses. "Have you seen the news?"

I sat at my desk with my laptop open beside me. "No. Why?"

"You should check it."

I moved the touch pad so the screen turned back on, and then I brought up my home page. "What am I looking for, Thorn?" If it was a natural disaster, those happened every day. If it was a murder, those happened too. Not much made me blink twice anymore.

"Hunt pulled out of the deal with Bruce Carol."

I heard the words but didn't process them as quickly as I usually did. Grabbing that lucrative company was a big deal, even for Hunt. Why would he squander it away when he had it in his grasp? "Why?"

"No idea. But Hunt made a statement saying he wouldn't do business with anyone who associates themselves with Bruce Carol...including buying his company."

All I could do was blink.

"And we both know...that affects everyone."

"Geez, what pissed him off?"

"I don't know," Thorn said. "But whatever it is, it's personal. He basically gave Bruce a death sentence."

Hunt was known for his brutality, and now I was seeing it firsthand.

"You need to talk to him about it, Titan. Because I want to know the dirt before you put another offer on the table."

That would be a nice perk of sleeping with Hunt, but it was a luxury I couldn't take advantage of. "I made it clear we wouldn't discuss business. In fact, I said that to him the last time we were together."

"But we can't make an offer without knowing what the problem is. For all we know, there's a huge problem in Bruce's company. But if there is no problem and Hunt just hates the guy, then we can get the company for an even lower price. Shit, you could basically just take it because Bruce will be so desperate without any other buyers. Hunt chased everyone away."

It was the perfect storm.

"You need to ask him, Titan. You know his fantasies —use them against him."

"I'm not going to manipulate him." I respected him way too much to play games. "If I want to know, I'll ask."

"Then ask."

I'd be going back on my word by opening up this topic, but even if I had no interest in the company, I wanted to know what Bruce had done to upset Hunt so severely. Did Bruce pull at a thread that made him come undone? Did he hit some invisible trigger? I cared because of Hunt—not what I would get out of it. "I'll think about it."

"You don't have much time to think about it," Thorn said over the phone. "I wouldn't wait longer than a day."

"We don't have any competition."

"But that can change," he said ominously. "We both know nothing is safe in our world."

WHEN I CAME HOME, THERE WAS A VASE OF FLOWERS waiting for me.

I picked up the card and read it.

Saw these beauties and thought of you.

XOXO,

Liv Cutler

I smiled then returned the card to the pick between the flowers. It was a clear vase full of pink peonies, and they looked beautiful. Thorn's mother knew I loved flowers because she shared the same passion. When I visited their place in Connecticut, she and I would garden together in the morning.

I slipped off my heels and let my thoughts turn back to Hunt. We hadn't spoken all day, and he must have figured out I knew about Bruce Carol's business by now. I wondered if he expected me to call.

Or not call.

Whether he told me what I wanted to know or not, I wanted him over here. I wanted that beautiful man to fuck me deep into my mattress, overpowering me with his brute strength and size.

I texted him. *Come over.*

I'm at the gym.

The bossy side of me came out. *I don't care where you are. I said come over.*

I pictured the smile on his face as he wrote back. *Yes, Boss Lady.*

Seeing him in a sweaty t-shirt sounded just as arousing as him in a suit. His muscles would be pumped with blood, thick and bulging. He'd already be worked up and ready to go, getting exercise from our romp in the sack. I loved it when sweat collected on his chest and his body had a nice sheen.

He walked inside ten minutes later, in black running shorts and a black t-shirt. The shirt was damp because it had absorbed his sweat. His hair was messy, probably from hitting the treadmill.

I thought he looked delicious.

"Here I am." He walked inside and set his gym bag on the floor near the elevator doors.

I was in the same black dress I wore to the office, something more expensive than the average person's mortgage. But I didn't care if it became damp in sweat— as long as it was Hunt's. "Hey." I moved into his chest and kissed him.

His hands were immediately in my hair as he kissed me back. He spoke between kisses. "Hey."

I kissed him longer than I planned, our kisses turning into a make-out session in front of the elevator doors. My hands shifted to the bottom of his shirt before I pulled it over his head, revealing his physique covered in a gleam of sweat. My hands moved over his chest, feeling the same slickness that I was used to in bed.

He moaned into my mouth before he tugged on the back of my hair. His hand slowly slid down my neck and to my back, discreetly grabbing my zipper and pulling it down to the top of my ass. The dress came loose and slowly slipped down my body. It dropped to my feet, surrounding my heels.

I got his shorts off next, and then we were in my bedroom. I lay naked on the sheets, my ass hanging over the edge.

He positioned himself between my legs, standing at the foot of the bed with his enormous cock laying against me. "How do you want it?"

"Slow and deep." I ran my hands up and down his chest. "I want to feel every inch of that big cock."

His eyes smoldered as they burned into mine. His hands slid up my stomach to my tits, where he grabbed each one in his big palms. He gave them a hard squeeze before his hands moved down again and back to my hips. "Yes, Boss Lady." He grabbed the backs of my knees and positioned my legs apart, opening me wide so he could take me good and hard. He thrust his hips and rubbed his length against my clitoris, making me shake even though I was already ready. He inserted two fingers inside me and gently pulsed as he leaned over me and kissed me.

I loved his warm fingers inside me, exploring how wet I was.

"God, you want me." His lips moved against mine as he spoke.

"Yes...all the time." My hands gripped his bulging arms, feeling the powerful muscles shift every time he moved.

After he explored me for a few seconds, he sucked my juice off his fingers and pointed his cock at my entrance. Like every time before, he had no problem sliding in, sinking deep inside my channel and squeezing my slit apart. He pushed until he was completely inside, his cock fully inserted.

I was so full, so tight, that I gripped his wrists and let out a moan.

He widened his stance and gripped the backs of my thighs, bringing himself to the perfect height above me. Then he started to move, giving me his entire length slowly before he pulled out again. He inserted himself again then pulled out, the tip of his cock remaining inside my soaked pussy each time before he pushed inside again.

"Hunt..."

He squeezed my thighs harder as he moved, hitting

me in the perfect spot each time. The sexiest part about the sex was the way he looked at me. With a jaw covered with coarse hair and those dark eyes, he stared at me ruthlessly. I could easily be on the other side of a conference table, a victim of those piercing coffee eyes. I could easily be his prey, with him taking exactly what he wanted from me without giving me a choice.

And I liked it.

I'd never enjoyed being overpowered by anyone, but it didn't feel so bad with Hunt.

My nipples hardened so much they actually hurt. My fingers dug into his skin and I nearly cut him, but I couldn't stop myself. I was on the verge of getting swept away by his tide, getting pulled under and drowning in pleasure. "Hunt...make me come."

He rubbed his thumb against my clitoris, applying pressure in a circular motion.

I liked to draw out my orgasms as much as possible, to make them build until they were white-hot, but now I was impatient. I wanted to come around Hunt's dick, to feel satisfied after missing him all day.

He quickened his pace slightly, his thumb working harder.

That was all I needed. "Yes..." I grabbed his hips and pulled him deeper into me, wanting every inch of his cock so I could come all around it. I wanted to surround him with my arousal, to make him understand just how good he made me feel. "God, yes."

He moved his cock in and out, soaked from the arousal my pussy produced. "My turn?" he asked with a husky voice and a sexy look.

I wanted him to experience the high I just felt, but I wasn't ready to end my own pleasure. I wanted his come, but not until the very end. And hearing him ask for my permission only heightened my love for power, for desperation, for control. "No. Not yet."

He dug his fingers into my thighs and growled.

"You'll come when I say so." I guided his hips into me, setting the particular pace I wanted. I knew exactly how I wanted to be fucked, and I wasn't ashamed to say so.

He moaned under his breath. "When it's my turn..." He didn't finish the sentence because he didn't need to. When he was the one in control and I had to obey, I knew he would do the same to me. He would torture me in many sexy ways, conquer me how he wanted and when he wanted.

And I'd have to obey.

WE BOTH GOT INTO THE SHOWER WHEN WE WERE

finished. I wiped myself down with a loofah, and Hunt rubbed a bar of soap into his skin. He dipped his head and let the water rinse away my shampoo before he stepped back and rubbed more soap into his body.

I felt his come slip between my legs and drip down my thigh.

Hunt spotted it, and he watched it with focused eyes. "Looks like I'll need to fill you up again before I leave."

"Fine with me."

He lathered my tits with soap and massaged them even though they were already clean. He squeezed them hard, making me wince slightly when he gripped me like a man gripped his woman. "I love your tits."

"They love you too."

He smiled before he clutched my ass. "What about her?"

"She's your biggest fan."

"And her?" His hand caressed my sex, and he slid a finger inside, getting his own come on his hand.

"You know how she feels about you…"

I turned off the water, and we each dried off with a towel. Hunt patted himself dry then scrubbed his hair with the towel, quickly drying it because his hair was so short. I had to use the hair dryer for a few minutes just so my hair wasn't so damp. When I was almost done, I was looking at my reflection in the mirror when Hunt appeared behind me. He was in his collared shirt and slacks, the same clothes he must have worn to work. He stood behind me and stared me down in the mirror.

I met his look, not standing down as I ran my fingers through my nearly dry hair. "What is it, Hunt?"

He pressed a kiss to my cheek, his eyes on me as he made the gesture. "I like the way you look without makeup." He turned around and walked out, leaving me alone to finish getting ready.

I was usually self-conscious without my makeup on, but I didn't think twice about it around him.

That was strange.

I pulled on jeans and a blouse, dressing up a little since he was still there. He might leave when I walked into the living room, but I wanted to be prepared for anything. I didn't put on any makeup, and not because of his compliment.

I just didn't feel like it.

He was sitting in the living room when I walked inside. "Would you like something to drink?"

"Please."

"What's your poison?"

"Water, please."

I poured two glasses and handed him one.

"Thanks."

I took a seat beside him on the couch, glad he didn't

leave right away. I still had to ask him about Bruce Carol, even though I wasn't entirely sure I was going to ask him about it at all.

A baseball game was on, so I turned up the volume.

"Are you a baseball fan?"

"Yep. Yankees."

"Hmm." He watched the TV as he sipped his water.

"Hmm, what?" I questioned.

"I didn't take you for a sports fan."

"Why?" I knew it wasn't because I was a woman. Hunt wasn't a sexist prick like most men.

"You don't seem like someone who has time to follow a sport."

"I usually have it on in the background, even if I'm working from home."

Hunt watched the TV again.

"What about you?"

"I like everything—except soccer. Never got into it."

"I hate golf. Bores me."

He chuckled. "That's not much fun to watch. But it's fun to play when you're doing business."

I'd had meetings on the links a few times. Men were always surprised I had my own set of clubs—and that I knew how to use them.

Hunt sat back against the cushions, getting comfortable on my couch. He looked at home there, his long legs separated and his glass of water sitting on the end table. His hair was still a little damp because it hadn't dried all the way, but the look was sexy on him. But then again, everything looked sexy on him.

My heart started to beat hard in my chest when I considered asking him about his falling out with Bruce Carol. I specifically said I didn't want to talk about business, but by bringing it up, I was going against my own decision.

But my curiosity was killing me.

If I'd lost a huge deal with a client, he would ask me about it too.

"I heard the news about you and Bruce."

Hunt didn't take his eye off the TV, but he clenched his jaw. "Yeah, I saw it on every channel. Didn't think it would get out that quickly."

"Well, your threat to everyone in the business world made everyone talk about it..." He basically promised to ruin anyone who got involved with Bruce Carol. For someone like Hunt, that didn't seem like a business practice he employed often. He usually stuck to himself, didn't air his dirty laundry for everyone to see. Whatever Bruce did, it was really bad.

"It was necessary." He rested one arm on the armrest while his other hand rested on his knee.

"What did he do to you?"

Hunt didn't say anything. He stared at the TV, his eyes following the players on the field until they got their last out. "I thought we didn't talk about business."

I thought he might use that against me, but I was still surprised when he did. At least I could tell Thorn I tried. "You're right, my mistake." I backed off, knowing I would get nowhere with Hunt.

I was naïve to think Hunt would treat me differently from the way I'd treated him.

When the game was over, he stood up. "I should get going. Pine, Mike, and I are going out."

"Okay." I walked him to the door and watched him pick up his bag.

That's when he noticed the vase of flowers on the table. He stared at them quietly, his eyes narrowing as he read the words on the card.

Talk about a breach of privacy. "Do you mind?"

His eyes shifted back to me, but now he looked angry. "If you cared enough, you should have put the card away."

"Does that mean I need to turn off my phone anytime I'm near you? If I get a text message, that gives you the right to read it?"

His angry face was nearly the same as his stoic face, but when he was pissed, his eyes were a little darker.

And he possessed this air of hostility...it was heavy in the air. "Not the same thing and you know it."

It wasn't, but I refused to admit that.

"Thorn's mother seems fond of you."

He connected the dots quickly. Must have seen that picture of the four of us having dinner. Goddamn social media. "She's a lovely person."

"And does she know you aren't really seeing Thorn?"

I'd told him this conversation wasn't up for discussion, but he constantly circled back to it. "I said I didn't want to talk about it, but you keep bringing it up. Why?"

"Because you expect me to trust you. How can I trust you when you're lying to the world?"

"I'm not lying," I argued.

"So you are seeing him?" he demanded.

"No..."

"Which is it?" he snapped. "Are you seeing Thorn, or aren't you?"

None of my other lovers was as bothered by Thorn as Hunt was. It got under his skin in a different way, probably because he was the biggest alpha I'd been with. "You don't need to concern yourself—"

"You're going to tell me."

My eyebrow cocked, shocked by his boldness.

"You're going to tell me because I have a right to know. We've got two more months of this. I already know you two have something going on, so there's not much more to hide. I could already expose you if I wanted, and of course, I won't. So why won't you tell me? You believe in trust so much? Prove it."

I crossed my arms over my chest, closing myself off from his hostility. Instead of being angry with his questions, I actually felt guilty. My personal life was none of his concern, but I didn't like seeing the doubt on his face —as if there was any chance I was screwing Thorn. "I'm not sleeping with him."

"That's not good enough for me."

Of course it wasn't. "Hunt, I would tell you, but it's not my secret to tell. Thorn asked me not to say anything to anyone."

"Except Pilar and Isa."

"That's different..."

"How?" he pressed.

"They're my friends."

"And I'm not?" he whispered. His eyes shifted back and forth as he looked into mine. "We can keep lying to each other, but I know there's something more than sex here. I admire you, I respect you, and as much as I hate to admit it, I care about you. I'm loyal to you when I'm not loyal to anyone else but myself. And call me crazy all you like, but I think you, Tatum Titan, feel the same way."

I felt my heart jump into my throat at the accusation, knowing he hit the truth right on the nose. He was right—dead on. I did see him as a friend. He hadn't stepped into my inner circle, but I did care about him. I saw him differently from the others. "You aren't crazy."

"I didn't think so. Now tell me."

I hesitated, my loyalty to Thorn unbreakable. "Let me talk to him again."

"No." All of his patience had disappeared the instant I called him a friend. "Give me the answer I want. And you can ask me one question in return—anything you want to know. I'll answer honestly."

When he offered, my heart skipped a beat. There was one thing I wanted to know—and Thorn wanted to know as well. Hunt would be willing to part with his secret in exchange for this important piece of knowledge. It could be worth a billion dollars. "You can't tell anyone, Hunt. I mean it."

He cocked his head to the side, his eyes drinking in mine. "You can trust me with all your secrets, Titan. I'll keep them safe. That's a promise."

I never trusted anyone, no matter what kind of pretty words they uttered, but I trusted Hunt. "Thorn and I have a special arrangement. We aren't seeing each other romantically. We've never slept together. But we're close friends...best friends. And one day, we're going to get married."

When Hunt heard what I said, he straightened his head and clenched his jaw slightly.

"I want to keep my sexual lifestyle, but I want to have kids someday. Thorn wants the same. In addition to that, we trust each other enough to combine our assets, to be business partners. He's not interested in love, and neither am I. It's the perfect arrangement for both of us."

Hunt finally got his answer, but he didn't have any response to it. He continued to stare at me with a tight jaw, his eyes as harsh as the scorching sun in the middle of the desert. "Do you love him?"

"As a friend, of course. I love him with all my heart."

"But are you in love with him?"

I shook my head. "No."

He rubbed the back of his neck, taking in the news slowly. "So, everyone thinks this is genuine? Including his parents?"

"Yeah."

He shook his head, as if he were disappointed.

"You don't have any right to judge me, Hunt." He had no idea what I'd endured, what I'd lost. There was no room in my heart for love ever again. I didn't trust anyone—and that would never change.

"I'm not judging," he whispered. "I just think you deserve more."

"I don't want anything more, Hunt. I want friendship, respect, and trust. I don't want romance. Not something I'm interested in."

He bowed his head, breaking eye contact. "When do you plan to marry him?"

"I don't know. When it's the right move for our careers."

He slipped his hands into his pockets and stepped back. "Thanks for answering my question."

"I told you that you had nothing to worry about."

"Actually...I have more to worry about now."

My eyes narrowed, unsure what that meant. "How so?"

"You're my friend, Titan. It's hard to stand there and watch your friend settle for less than what they deserve."

"I assure you I don't want romance. Of all people, I thought you would understand that."

"Why would I?"

"You don't seem like the marriage kind of guy."

He shrugged. "I'm not against it. The door is always open for the possibility. I'm not closing it by marrying some woman I don't love."

I was tired of talking about this. We obviously had a

difference of opinion that couldn't be rectified. "Can I ask my question now?"

"Fire away."

"Why did you pull out of the deal with Bruce Carol?"

He smiled, but it wasn't the genuine kind that I liked.

"What?"

"Nothing," he said quickly. "I pulled out of the deal because Bruce and I weren't compatible."

"But it's not like you would be working with him."

"I offered five percent of my profits to him in the deal."

That was something I would never offer him.

"And I wasn't giving any of my profits to a man that I despise."

"So it had nothing to do with the company itself?"

"Not at all. If you still want it, make sure you give him the lowest offer possible. Lowball the shit out of him, Titan." He spoke with a hard jaw, his words coming out harsh.

"What did he say to you, Hunt?"

"You really want to know?"

I wanted to know what Bruce could possibly say to make Hunt this upset. "Yes."

He regarded me for a long time before he answered. "I'm not going to repeat it. But he said some very disrespectful things about you...things that made my blood boil."

The words took a few seconds to sink into my body. When they finally dissolved in my bloodstream, my throat felt dry. I couldn't believe Bruce Carol said something so offensive after I made him a fair offer. My intuition was correct when I met him—he didn't respect me at all. "What did he say?"

Hunt shook his head slightly.

"Answer me."

He sighed. "He said he would never give his company to a woman...but he would reconsider if you sucked his dick first."

Fucking pig.

Only a small man would make comments like that.

"And he thought you had an ass like a nectarine."

I kept a straight face and pretended this information didn't bother me, but it burned me to the bone. I worked hard to be respected, to be twice as savvy as my competitors. I always treated everyone with respect, even if they didn't treat me the same way. To constantly take the high road and never be respected for it was exhausting. No matter my intelligence or my success, I would always be second best—and mocked. "You shouldn't walk away from his company because of me, Hunt. There's a lot of money on the table."

"Money isn't everything."

"All men speak about me that way. It just comes with the territory."

"I've never said anything like that about you—or any woman."

"Well...you're one of the few."

His expression slowly began to soften as sympathy moved into his features. "You're my friend, Titan. I don't let people talk about my friends like that and get away with it. When I said I admired you, I meant it. You're smarter than you let on, you're fiercer than I am, and you're a hustler. Ten years from now, you're probably going to pass me on the Forbes List. And the day you do...I'll smile."

Now I really struggled to keep my features stoic, to hide the impact his words had on me. He spoke directly to the core of my insecurities, to the vulnerable part of me that was constantly wounded.

"You deserve more respect than you're given. I'll always stand up for you—because it's the right thing to do."

"Hunt..." My voice came out weak, hitting a pitch I'd never reached before. "No one has ever said that to me before..."

His hand moved to my cheek as he cupped my face. "That's gonna change. I promise."

My fingers wrapped around his wrist, and I looked into his handsome face, touched by this man in a way I'd never been touched before. I loved everything about him, from his warm caress to his beautiful smile. He possessed the kind of strength I'd never achieve, the kind of power that came from somewhere else besides between his legs.

"Get that company, Titan. And take everything he's got." He pushed his mouth to mine and gave me a soft kiss before he stepped away, getting ready to walk out of my penthouse. He hit the button on the wall, and the doors opened.

A thought came into my mind, and I couldn't believe I was going to say it. It went against everything I believed in, against the rules I set out the day I turned fifteen. "Hunt?"

He held the door open as he looked at me. "Hmm?"

"I'm gonna buy that company from Bruce. But I want to split it with you."

He kept his arm against the elevator door as he looked at me, a slow smile stretching over his lips. "You want to be a partner with me."

"Yeah. I think we'd be great together."

"I know that isn't the way you do things. And frankly, it's not the way I do things either."

"Maybe it's time we make a change...because we deserve more."

Now he smiled wide, possessing boyish charm and manly strength. "Maybe you're right."

Thorn walked into his living room in just his sweatpants and bare feet. His hair was messy like a woman had been running her fingers through it all night.

That was probably exactly what had happened.

"How'd it go with Hunt?" He poured two mugs of coffee and came into the living room. He sat beside me and took a long drink of his coffee, trying to wake up. He rubbed the sleep from the corner of his eye, his chin covered with stubble.

"Well."

"Yeah? Are we gonna make an offer."

"I'll meet with Bruce on Monday."

"Then Hunt didn't step away because of the company?"

"No. He stepped away for another reason."

"Which was...?" He gave me an irritated look before he drank his coffee again.

"Apparently, Bruce made some derogatory

comments about me. It pissed Hunt off, so he called off the whole thing."

Thorn was mid-drink when he pulled the mug way. "Bruce did what?" he asked incredulously. "What did he say?"

"That he would only sell his company to me if I sucked his dick." I said it with a straight face, refusing to let a small man like Bruce Carol bother me. Why should I care what he thought about me? He was the one about to file for bankruptcy, not me. "And I have an ass like a nectarine."

Thorn's nostrils flared just like a bull about to jump out of the chute. The vein in his forehead began to throb, and he turned so angry in such a short amount of time. His fuse was short, and the dynamite went off. "Fucking piece of shit."

Hunt had been just as livid if he'd backed out of the deal and declared war against him. "I don't think it's worth getting upset about."

"Not worth getting upset about? Who the hell does he think he is?"

"Nobody," I said simply. "That's why we're buying him out—because we're somebody."

Thorn softened slightly. "I'm surprised Hunt did that."

"I'm not." He was cold and callous on the surface, but there was beautiful beating heart underneath.

Thorn studied me with slight eyebrow raise. "You aren't?"

"He's a nice guy."

"I'm a nice guy too, but I'm not so sure I would have done the same thing."

"I don't believe that for a second."

"I would do it for you, obviously. But not some woman I'm just fucking. Wouldn't feel the need to defend her honor and walk away from a shit-ton of money unless she meant something to me..." The look he gave me was full of accusation.

"What's that supposed to mean?"

"You're too smart to play dumb," he snapped. "You know exactly what it means."

"Hunt doesn't see me like that. He cares about me and sees me as a friend, but that's it."

Thorn looked away and drank from his mug again. "What now?"

"I'm gonna make an offer—but Hunt and I are going in together."

Now Thorn looked angry all over again. "What?"

"I had to do it, Thorn."

"Did he make you?" he asked incredulously. "Nobody makes Tatum Titan do shit."

"I offered—since he did that for me."

He sighed and ran his fingers through his hair. "I know you wanna show your appreciation because of what he did, but there are other ways to do that—which you're already doing."

"I already made the offer, and he accepted it."

"Titan, it's just supposed to be the two of us."

"I'm just splitting one company with him. It has nothing to do with my other businesses. There's only money to be made, not lost."

"You've never partnered with anyone before."

"There's a first time for everything."

"And he hasn't either."

"Great minds think alike..."

He ran his fingers through his hair again, obviously annoyed by this turn of events.

Since he was already annoyed, I decided to keep piling it on to get it over with. "I told him about us."

Thorn turned back to me, wearing a shocked expression. "What does that mean?"

"He told me I had to tell him if I wanted to know the truth about Bruce Carol. I wasn't going to get that information any other way."

"So he blackmailed you?"

"No. You need to look up the word because you obviously don't know what it means."

His eyes narrowed. "Titan, I'm not in the mood for your smartass comments today."

Neither was I.

"That was supposed to stay between us." He pointed from me to himself.

I nodded toward his bedroom. "And what do your girls think? You're just a cheating liar?"

"I don't care what they think."

"Hunt was already onto us. He'd asked me about it at least five times."

"Seems overly invested in your personal relationship..."

"I think he was just afraid you and I were sleeping together."

He rolled his eyes. "I made it clear to him I didn't care that you were sleeping with him, so that doesn't make sense."

"He's a paranoid man, just like I'm a paranoid woman."

He pinched the bridge of his nose. "Whatever."

"He won't say anything, Thorn. I trust him."

"You've only known him for a few months."

"I just know," I said confidently. "Besides, after we get married, I'm gonna have to tell my lovers anyway. The last thing I want for people to think is that I'm a liar."

Thorn didn't argue that point because there was nothing to say. People were going to know the truth about our relationship whether we liked it or not. There was no fighting it.

Thorn sighed again before he finally relaxed. "Now what?"

"I'm gonna move forward with Hunt."

"You don't think that will be a conflict of interest when your relationship ends?"

"We'll end on positive terms. We agreed to six weeks each. Nothing more. If anything, I think it'll bring us closer together."

The bedroom door opened, and a pretty blonde stepped out into the hallway. She was in just Thorn's white t-shirt. With messy hair and smeared makeup, she looked like she'd had a good night. She stopped when she saw me, obviously uncomfortable with my presence.

"We're just finishing up, baby," Thorn said. "I'll be right there."

She walked back into the bedroom. The door clicked shut behind her.

Thorn grinned. "She's like a wild animal. Rode me like a pro."

I chuckled. "Good to know. Looked like she recognized me."

"Most of them do. But I'll assure her it's cool."

"Well, I'll get out of your hair." I rose to my feet, and Thorn walked me to the door, his chiseled physique like moving rocks. He was all muscle and skin—nothing else.

"Let me know how it goes on Monday."

"I will. By the way, your mother sent me flowers. Peonies."

He chuckled. "My mom loves you more than me."

"Can't blame her—you're a shithead."

He smiled as he slid his arm around my waist. "When I was little, I always wondered what my wife would be like. I hoped she'd be hot, funny, smart...you know. But you exceed every expectation I've ever had—minus being a smartass."

"Don't act like you don't love that about me." I gave him a gentle pat on the cheek before I walked out.

He called after me. "You know what, you really do have an ass like a nectarine."

I turned around and flipped him the bird.

He chuckled and shut the door.

6

HUNT

I'D ONLY BEEN SITTING at my desk for ten minutes when Natalie spoke to me through the intercom. "Sir, Thorn Cutler is here to see you. Doesn't have an appointment, but said I should relay the message to you."

Thorn would only be here for one reason—Titan. She must have told him that I knew about their secret deal. He probably came to threaten me to be quiet.

I'd threaten him back.

"Send him in."

A minute later, Thorn walked through the door. In a gray suit and black tie, he walked inside with one hand in his pocket. He had light brown hair that was almost blond, pretty blue eyes that the women must love, and an arrogant smile that annoyed me. He walked up to my desk, didn't shake my hand, and took a seat.

I eyed my watch on my wrist. "I don't have a lot of time, Thorn. Say what you need to say."

"I won't be long." He tapped his fingers against the armrest.

It didn't seem that way. "I told Titan I wouldn't share your secret. You don't need to be concerned about it."

"I'm not," he said. "You seem like an honorable guy. I'm concerned about something else entirely."

I sat back, resting my ankle on the opposite knee. My fingertips came together in my lap, studying him like he was a buck while I was holding a shotgun. "I'm listening."

"Titan told me a few things...and I'd be lying if I said I wasn't concerned. She assured me there was nothing to worry about, but I'm not so certain."

Was it because we were going into business together?

"I don't think a man would walk away from easy money the way you did with Bruce Carol without a strong reason to..." He studied me the same way I studied him, like he was also a hunter.

But I would never be prey. "You should speak your mind and save us both time, Thorn."

He leaned forward, resting his elbows on his thighs. "I also don't see why a man would care so much about what I mean to Titan...unless he had a reason to."

Did he speak to Titan like this all the time? That would drive her crazy after the first thirty seconds.

"It seems like you care more about Titan than you should." He stared me down with his crystal blue eyes, appearing threatening without changing his expression. He rested his fingertips against his chin.

I didn't respond because I had nothing to say to that statement.

"Women like Titan don't exist. She's the only one of her kind, a special breed. But make no mistake—she's mine." He pointed his fingers at his chest.

My blood started to boil.

"I'm not fucking her. I'm not in love with her. But she's mine. She's going to be my wife and the mother of my kids, the ultimate business partner. I'm gonna give you the benefit of the doubt and assume you're just a genuinely nice guy that sticks up for the underdog...but I don't want there to be a misunderstanding between us."

I hadn't minded Thorn initially.

He didn't seem like a threat.

But now I hated him. I hated him, and I didn't understand why.

"When your arrangement is over, that's it. You move on."

All I could do was stare.

Thorn waited for me to say something, and when I didn't, he spoke again. "Tell me I'm wrong, Hunt. I want to be wrong."

"I think marrying her is a mistake."

"For her or for me?"

"Both of you," I said simply. "She deserves something real."

"I am real. Other than my fidelity, she'll have everything else. I'll be the one to take care of her when she gets sick. I'll be the one to grow old and gray with her. I'll be a great father. I'll love her every single day—in my own way."

"Titan deserves the best. We both know you aren't it."

His eyes narrowed. "Are you saying my assumption is correct?"

I understood the parameters of our relationship. I wasn't looking for anything more than good sex. What we had was good enough for me, and like all things, I would eventually grow tired of it. But Titan had changed my life in many ways—for the better. I gained a friend, a confidant. "No, your assumption is not correct."

Thorn leaned back into the chair, visibly relaxing.

"I respected Titan the moment I looked at her. I even admired her. I feel my fondness grow for her."

A smile formed. "She has that effect on people."

"And I hope to be a good friend of hers as time goes on. But no, I'm not trying to keep her." At the moment, I didn't want anyone else. She was the only woman I wanted to be with, the sex absolutely incredible. She pleased me in a way no one else ever had. But like all things, I would grow tired of it. That was just how my personality was, as much as I wished I were different. My high would wear off, and I would crave someone else—no matter how amazing as Titan was. The only time someone stayed in my life was if they were a friend. And if Titan became my friend, I would keep her a lot longer that way.

Thorn looked satisfied with that answer. "Then we don't have a problem." He rose to his feet and walked to the edge of my desk. He extended his hand.

I almost didn't shake it. While our conversation had ended positively, I still despised him. I didn't like the fact that he got to keep Titan for the rest of his life, that he somehow had talked her into this idiotic arrangement. "Why does she want this?" I stood up but didn't shake his hand. "Is it because her boyfriend died? She thinks she could never fall in love again?" Had she given up on that kind of happiness?

Thorn's face turned as pale as milk. Slowly, his hand went down until it returned to his side. He didn't blink once as he looked at me, neither angry nor upset. He was stoic, having no visible emotion at all.

I'd never seen him react that way. He had expressive eyes and a distinctive body language, but now he wasn't giving any signals at all.

"Don't ever mention that to her." His voice barely came out as a whisper. "This is something you don't comprehend, so don't bother trying to understand it. It's none of your business, so stay the fuck out of it."

I'd crossed a line with the question—making Thorn angry in a way I'd never seen. Both of his arms were shaking slightly, barely noticeable tremors. He hadn't blinked yet, his eyes wide open like an owl.

"Bring it up to her, and I'll fucking kill you." He left my office and walked to the door. He gave me one more violent look before he walked out. "Fucking kill you."

I'D JUST FINISHED WITH A CALL WHEN TITAN'S NAME appeared on my phone. She was calling me directly, skipping the office phone because she had access to me in ways most people didn't. When I saw her name, I naturally smiled. But that smirk faded away when I remembered my final conversation a few hours ago. I answered. "Titan."

Her smile was loud through the phone. "Hunt."

She never called me by my first name. I was certain I hadn't heard it on her lips before. Most people didn't, so that wasn't unusual. "Have I ever told you that you have the sexiest voice?"

"If you think my voice is sexy, you should see my panties."

My hand immediately formed a fist at her quick comeback. It was witty and sexy. Now I pictured her in the black lingerie I'd last seen her in, her tits pushed together, hard and perky. She took control and dominated me, making my fantasies come true. While I enjoyed every second of it, my submission was beginning to wane. I wanted to be the one to conquer her, to order her to her knees every time I walked in the room. Her need for control was simply about her need for power, to issue the orders. My need for control was something completely different. I wanted to master her in the sexiest way possible, to bring the most powerful woman to her knees with a single command. I wanted to own her in a way no other man had—including Thorn Cutler. "I would love to see your panties."

"I thought you might. We should discuss our plan for Bruce Carol. Come to my office."

Her bossiness was sexy, but also irritating. I put up with it because I would be rewarded in the end. Obeying her would all be worth it just to watch her obey me. "Let's talk over lunch. I haven't eaten."

"I can have my assistant run out and pick up something."

I'd never eaten with her in a restaurant—alone. There was always someone joining us. I could try to override her, but since she was in charge, I yielded. "You have glass doors on your office." I didn't need to be more specific to explain what I was thinking.

"We have the rest of the day, Hunt. I'll see you soon." Like our conversation was over, she hung up.

I couldn't wipe the smile off my face as I set my phone down. That woman owned every room she walked into—even if she wasn't physically in the room.

As soon as I arrived at her office, her assistant ushered me through the glass doors.

Titan was at her massive white desk, writing with a matching white pen. A vase of peonies was sitting on the corner, bright and pink. They were the very ones Thorn's mother sent her.

I swallowed my annoyance.

"Hello, Hunt. Take a seat. I'm just finishing something up..."

I eyed the table that had been rolled inside. Lunch was set up, two salads, sandwiches, a bowl of fruit, and two Old Fashioneds. She balanced her liquor addiction with low-calorie options. She watched her weight, which was how she looked so sexy all the time. But she couldn't give up her poison altogether.

I respected that.

I took a seat and waited for her to finish.

When she was done, she walked up to me and extended her hand to shake mine.

I eyed it, refusing to give the gesture. "Shaking hands is beneath us, Titan."

"Anytime we aren't alone, we're being watched." She narrowed her green eyes at me. "So shake my hand."

I finally did as she asked, controlling my smile the best I could. But I squeezed her hand a little tighter than I usually would, silently telling her I wished I were squeezing something else.

After she achieved my cooperation, she took the seat across from me. She was in a black dress with a V neck in the front, along with a white gold chain around her throat. Her nails were painted with French tips, and the delicate muscles of her arms showed her body's tightness. She set her cloth napkin on her lap then dug into her salad.

I studied her, watching her painted lips open as she

placed the food into her mouth. Whenever I saw her, I was always greeted with a kiss—on my mouth or my dick. I didn't like the professionalism of this meeting, being treated like I was a business associate instead of her lover.

If we were in my office, I would be fucking her right now.

"I haven't scheduled a meeting with Bruce yet." If she knew I was staring at her, she ignored it. She must be used to my intense gaze by now. And I probably wasn't the only man who stared at her intently.

"You want me to handle it?"

"That's not what I said." She picked at her salad, eating a few bites here and there. But most of her energy went to her Old Fashioned.

I didn't mention Thorn stopping by my office that morning. It would probably make her angry with him if she knew he'd pulled that stunt, but I still kept it to myself. I'd feel like a rat if I said anything. "Bruce Carol knows he doesn't have any options now. No one else will make a move—fearful of my wrath." I'd basically dropped my pants and told the world I had the biggest dick.

"Maybe we should stop by together—without a meeting."

It wasn't professional to stop by unannounced, but it

also wasn't professional to talk about making a woman suck your dick either. He didn't deserve our respect. Titan and I only wanted to conquer, to take him for everything that he had. "No warning. I like it." I grabbed my fork and took a bite.

"We sweep him clean. He'll take whatever we offer because he won't have much of a choice."

"Exactly."

She took a bite of her sandwich, her small lips moving slowly as she chewed.

I watched every move she made. "You want to do this now?"

"The longer we wait, the worse our deal's gonna be."

"True." She threw her napkin on the table, her plate just as full as when it arrived.

Come to think of it, I'd never seen her finish a meal. The only thing I ever saw her complete was an old-fashion—several of them.

"Let's get going." She rose from her chair and grabbed her clutch from her desk.

I stared at her ass, noticing how tight it looked in her skirt. I almost couldn't blame Bruce for his asshole comment. Now I was staring at her ass just as hard. But the difference between us was I had her explicit permission.

She turned around, catching my gaze as it shifted back to her face.

She didn't care at all. "Unless you have a busy day."

I got out of my chair and set the napkin on the table. "I always have a busy day. I'll tell Natalie to cancel everything this afternoon."

"So you're ready to do this now?"

I slid my hands into my pockets, hating the glass doors right behind me. I didn't like being in public. This woman turned me into a different man, but I couldn't let that man come out when there were so many witnesses. "Absolutely. But are you sure you want to do business with a jackass like him? Wouldn't blame you if you didn't."

"I don't care what he thinks of me. He can continue to be the egotistical, sexist pig all he wants. I'm laughing all the way to the bank."

WE WAITED IN THE LOBBY TEN MINUTES BEFORE BRUCE would see us. He'd had a short warning, but not enough to truly prepare for our meeting. Besides, he had no way to prepare for what was about to happen. His empire was slowly sinking into the ground, and he was desperately trying to jump ship—but there was nowhere to land.

I sat beside Titan with my hands in my lap. My ankle rested on the opposite knee, and every time I looked up, Bruce's assistant was watching me. She held my gaze for a split second before she looked down. Red cheeks followed afterward, along with a smile. She was a pretty girl, but she didn't command my attention the way Titan did.

Titan sat beside me with her legs crossed. She sat perfectly straight, her back as rigid as a flat piece of wood. Her hair was in soft curls, and she wore dark makeup around her eyes. Instead of looking like a CEO, she looked like a model.

Anytime I was beside her, I was conscious of our proximity. I was more aware of my lips than usual, feeling their softness and plumpness with my tongue. They felt lonely when they weren't pressed to Titan's mouth—or any other part of her body.

I'd worked with beautiful women on a daily basis, and I never experienced this kind of struggle. As natural as it was to breathe, I felt the need to place my hand on her thigh and let it rest there.

I'd never done it to her before, but the urge was so normal that it felt like I'd done it a hundred times.

I wanted to drape my arm over the back of her chair

and lean toward her to whisper something in her ear. The words didn't come to mind, but maybe I didn't need words at all. I could press my lips to the shell of her ear and just remain there, listen to her breath as it quickened in anticipation of my touch.

I was just about to land a huge business deal—but all I could think about was Tatum Titan.

Did she feel the same distraction I did? Did she feel the magnetic pull between us?

When I glanced at her legs, I saw them reposition, rubbing together.

I had my answer.

Bruce's assistant came to us in the waiting room. "Mr. Carol will see you now."

I buttoned the front of my suit as I stood, ready to tango with the devil. I hadn't considered how I would feel coming face-to-face with him after the last time he spoke to me. I wanted to murder him for insulting Titan so inappropriately. Just because I was making a deal with him now didn't mean my feelings had changed.

I was glad Titan was going to walk in there with her head held high. She seemed less affected by the insults than I was. She took them in stride, refusing to let them drag her down. She was too powerful, too pure for that. Unlike most businessmen, she didn't have time to feel hurt. She just wanted to get the job done.

We walked together down the same hallway we'd both taken before—but this time together and not separately. When I saw her walk out of Bruce's office initially, I was both shocked and unsurprised. I didn't know how she'd figured out Bruce was ready to be bought out, but it didn't surprise me how quickly she jumped on the opportunity. In fact, she'd beat me to it.

Just before we reached the door, my hand moved to the small of her back, and I pressed my mouth to her ear. "I'll let you lead. I know you'll give him hell." I pulled my arm away just before we stepped inside, returning to a mere business partner and not a lover.

Titan brushed it off like it never happened. "Mr. Carol." She walked up to the desk, set down her folder, and took a seat. She didn't bother walking around the table to shake his hand. Her hands came together in front of her, staring him down like he was something beneath her.

I took the seat beside her, my allegiance abundantly clear. I rested my hands on my lap, looking at the puffy old man sitting across from us. He wasn't as jolly this time around. His eyes kept moving to Titan, ignoring me altogether.

"Mr. Hunt and I are here to make you an offer." Titan opened her portfolio, pulled out the sheet of paper that we agreed to hand over, and slid it across the table.

Bruce didn't reach for it, letting it sit in front of him.

"Unfortunately," she said, "there will be no blow job as part of the deal."

I did my best not to smile.

"You're going to sell it to me anyway, at half the price I initially offered you. Take what you can get and walk away."

Bruce took a breath before he pulled the paper toward him. He hadn't spoken the entire time, too cowardly to say anything. He browsed through the paper before he set it down again.

"Do you accept our offer?"

Bruce looked at me when he spoke. "No. I want—"

"I don't give a damn what you want." Titan didn't raise her voice, but her presence suddenly felt larger than it had before. She took up most of the room, even making me feel small. "We're the only offer you have. And just for the hesitation, I'm taking it down by ten percent."

Don't smile. Don't smile. Don't smile.

Bruce's jaw nearly dropped. "Are you out of—"

"It just turned into twenty percent. Think wisely before you speak again." Titan didn't need me to say anything at all. She had this deal in the bag. She could run a meeting better than a drill sergeant could hustle his soldiers.

Bruce's mouth opened, but he abruptly closed it again, thinking to himself. He rubbed his jaw, his fingers tracing his mustache. He said something under his breath before he looked at Titan again. "Fine."

Like the lady she was, she didn't gloat about robbing a man with his eyes wide open. She opened her folder, pulled out the paperwork, and crossed out the incorrect numbers since the offer had spiraled down. She pushed it toward him. "You know where to sign, Bruce."

Bruce grabbed his pen and took his time signing, his hand shaking slightly.

Titan watched him with her hands on the desk.

But I watched her. Titan worked him hard—like a boss.

When Bruce finished signing the paperwork, he pushed everything back to her.

"Great." Titan gathered everything before she stood up. "The money will be in your account shortly. I expect all of your things to be removed by tomorrow morning —your employees can stay."

I pulled out Titan's chair as she stood before I did the same.

She walked off first but turned around when she reached the door. "I don't have an ass like a nectarine, Mr. Carol." Her green eyes looked terrifying as she stared him down, her soft hair unable to make her look more feminine because she was so hard in that moment. With a rigid posture and a queenly authority, she took control of the room. She even took control of me because I couldn't take my eyes off her. "But I do have an ass that won't quit."

WE SAT TOGETHER IN THE BACK SEAT AS HER DRIVER drove us back to her office. There was a solid divider between us and the driver, along with black-tinted windows all around the black Mercedes. It was similar to mine, something good enough for the President of the United States if he ever needed a ride.

Titan was still rigid, like there were unfriendly eyes watching her now.

I slid my hand across the seat and up her thigh until my hand found hers. I intertwined our fingers together, my hands twice the size of hers. I gripped her gently, looking down at her. Now that we were alone together, I could finally stare at her as much as I wanted. If she didn't object to it, I'd fuck her in the back seat right now.

Her hand squeezed me back.

"You were a badass in there."

She turned her head my way, a small smile on her lips. "Yeah?"

I whistled quietly. "I wanted to fuck you on that desk then and there."

"You'd want to fuck me on that desk anyway."

An unstoppable smile stretched across my lips. "Good point."

"You don't think I'm too bossy?" She'd never asked for my opinion before. This was a first.

"Not any bossier than I am."

"Think I'm too forward?"

"I like it when you're forward." I brought her hand to my lips and kissed her knuckles. "I like how powerful you are, how hard you are. You know exactly what you want, and you aren't afraid to ask for it. Demand it, actually. Sexiest thing I've ever seen in my life."

"Really?" she whispered. "Most men don't see it that way."

Titan had just peeled back another layer to me, admitting that she was actually self-conscious about who she was. I suspected she didn't even say these things to Thorn. Obviously, she felt comfortable with me, in the same way I felt comfortable with her.

"Bruce will tell everyone I'm a bitch in stilettos." Her voice remained controlled and she didn't seem upset, but I detected the hint of sorrow behind her bold words.

That's when I realized she was actually hurt by what Bruce had said. "Look at me."

She didn't.

"Titan." I inserted more authority into my voice, daring her to defy me. She might have all the control in this relationship, but I took back the power once it was necessary.

She slowly turned her head my way, looking at me with guarded eyes.

"Men only say that shit because they're intimidated by you."

"Are you intimidated by me?"

My smile was my response. "Never. But real men aren't threatened by successful women. Real men are secure in their own success and their own masculinity not to think twice about working with a woman like you. They give the same respect they feel they're due. Don't ever let scumbags like him make you second-guess yourself. You're too way too good for that." I leaned in and kissed her, my palm caressing her cheek.

She kissed me back, her fingers still exploring my wrist. "Hunt...you aren't what I expected at all."

"How so?" I whispered against her mouth.

"I never expected to like you so much...to enjoy you so much."

I looked into her eyes before I rubbed my nose against hers. "We have a lot in common, Titan. We're two sides of the same coin."

"We are." I brushed my thumb against her cheek before I kissed her again. "I hope when this is over, you still consider me to be your friend. Because you've become very important to me."

Her eyes softened as she looked into my eyes. "You're a great friend to me, Hunt. Now that we're running a business like this together, we're gonna be more than friends."

My eyes narrowed on hers. "We are?"

"Yes." She kissed my mouth gently. "We'll be business partners."

I DIDN'T WANT TO GO OUT TONIGHT, BUT I DIDN'T HAVE A choice.

I'd blown off Pine and Mike too many times now.

We hit the club scene, found some women, and then barhopped until we found the perfect booth for the night. I had a girl under each arm, and every time they tried to kiss me, I discreetly turned away and took a drink of my Old Fashioned.

Yes, Old Fashioneds were my drink now.

"You and Titan are business partners now?" Pine asked incredulously. "How did that happen?"

"I thought you didn't partner with anyone," Mike noted.

One of the girls leaned into me and dragged her hand down my chest.

I didn't like it.

Titan couldn't get upset if I kissed a woman. I had to keep up pretenses somehow. She wouldn't let me tell my closest friends about her, so she would have to deal with it. But once I smelled foreign perfume and came close to their lipstick, I turned away.

I didn't want it.

"Titan isn't just some partner," I said. "She's the best."

"Still," Pine said. "You've had the opportunity with richer men, but you never went for it. You said you would always fly solo."

Mike held his hand in the air and made it look like a plane flying about.

"Business is an evolving game," I said simply. "I had to adapt."

"You had that shit in the bag," Pine said. "Then you pulled out...and then you went in again. I don't get it."

I didn't tell them what Bruce said. The more people knew about it, the more people would mock Titan for it. So I kept that info to myself. "Titan and I managed to get him to half of what my original offer was. Only she could have made that happen."

"Half?" Pine asked incredulously. "That's a significant difference."

"A big difference." I picked up my glass to take a drink, but one of the girls took it away from me. She batted her eyelashes flirtatiously before she brought the glass to her lips to take a drink.

I smiled even though I was fiercely annoyed.

"Are you sure you can work with Titan every day?" Pine asked incredulously. "I hear that—"

"Be very careful, Pine." I didn't give a damn if he was my friend. I didn't want to hear anything negative about Titan. She worked too hard, was too smart, to be disrespected so easily. I warned him with my eyes, telling him I wasn't joking around.

Pine's eyes narrowed. "You still have a thing for her? Is that what all of this is about?"

"You think if you run a business with her, you'll finally get between her legs?" Mike asked. "Damn, I like pussy as much as the next person, but not that much."

"Talk about her pussy again and see what happens." I clenched my jaw and focused my hatred on Mike.

Mike leaned back and put his hands up in surrender. "Alright, sorry."

My life would be so much easier if I could just tell

them the truth. We wouldn't have to have these stupid conversations about her. They would know she was my friend as well as the woman I was bedding.

But Titan was a pain in the fucking ass.

As if she knew she was the subject for the night, she texted me. *Come over and fuck me. Now.*

Jesus Christ. This woman could get me hard in record time. My cock pressed against the zipper of my slacks, and my chest ached with the deep breath I took. *I'm out with the guys right now.*

I don't give a damn what you're doing.

She was killing me.

Get over here now. Don't make me ask you again.

I wanted her to ask me again. *I'll be there in an hour or so.*

You just earned yourself a slap.

My cheek burned where she would hit me when I arrived. I loved that little palm against my face. She could pack an impressive hit when she tried. My body hummed to life when I pictured her smacking me. It turned me on in a way I couldn't explain. I was the most ambitious man in the world, and I was attracted to power.

And Titan was the most powerful woman in the world.

No wonder why I wanted her so much.

I'm on my way.

She texted back immediately. *That's what I thought.*

THE INSTANT I STEPPED THROUGH THE ELEVATOR DOORS, she slapped me.

And she slapped me hard.

I turned with the heat, feeling my blood flood with adrenaline. I was turned on before the doors opened, but now I wanted her even more. Something about that palm drove me wild. I wanted her to hit me until my face was swollen for a week.

She stood in just a black bra and matching panties, looking sexy as hell with her curled hair and heavy eye makeup. She looked lustrous, like a model inside a lingerie catalog. She had a slender waistline and noticeable abs along her stomach. She wasn't just thin, but toned. However, I didn't have a clue when she had time to exercise.

My arousal took over, and I rushed her, charging her against the wall of the living room until her back smacked against it. I scooped her up in my powerful arms and kissed her, my teeth knocking against hers because I was more aggressive than usual.

That's what her slaps did to me.

She clawed at my back and breathed into my mouth, her moans silenced by my lips. Her heels dug into my ass, and she held herself up.

After minutes of heated embraces, she wrapped her arms around my neck and pulled away. "You like it when I slap you, don't you?"

I sucked her bottom lip into my mouth. "What gave me away?"

"Then you'll like everything else I have planned for you." She gripped my body as she lowered herself to the ground. She purposely halted our sexy embrace, walking away from me in her sky-high heels.

I stared at her luscious ass. I couldn't wait until I got to spank it.

She stopped when she was several feet away from me, purposely keeping distance between us.

Why did she call me over here just to torture both of us?

She placed her hands on her hips as she looked at me, her hair trailing over both of her shoulders. She wore a white gold necklace with a diamond pendant in the center. Her skin was tanned and soft, about to be kissed by my aching mouth. "I've tried to come up with a way to properly thank you for what you did for me."

I didn't do anything for her. If she was referring to

standing up to Bruce Carol, I didn't do that for her. I did that for myself.

"But you're a man who already has everything he could ever want. What could I possibly offer you?"

You.

"So I decided to do something special for you." She slowly walked back toward me, her heels tapping against the hardwood floor.

I felt hot in these clothes. They should be in a pile on the floor. My cock should be wild and free, ready to fuck her. "What is that?"

"I'll fulfill whatever fantasy you want. Tell me what you like, and I'll do it for you."

"I get to choose?"

"Yes. You don't have the control, but you get the option." She closed the gap between us and ran her hands up my chest. She slowly undid each button of my shirt until it was open against my chest. Her hands worked my belt and zipper, getting them loose. "So what do you want, Hunt?"

Every time we were together, it was as good as the last. She fucked as well as she ran her empire. It was second nature to her, and I'd never met another woman who knew how to please herself so well—as well as her partner. There was never anything she did that I didn't love. Even when she tortured me by not allowing me to have a climax when I felt like it, it was still amazing.

She pushed my shirt over my shoulders, her eyes on my lips. "How do you want me to fuck you, Hunt?" She kneeled down and pulled my slacks and boxers down as well. When my shoes were off and my clothes were abandoned on the hardwood floor, I was naked from top to bottom.

My cock was pulsing.

She moved into my chest and tilted her face up so she could kiss me. "Tell me, Hunt."

I had a list that was too long to repeat. I knew exactly what I wanted to do with her once she was mine—down to the last detail. I would dominate her in a way she'd never known. I would rule her, make her my pawn. But that wasn't for another three weeks. "I want you to dance for me."

Her mouth paused against mine. "Dance for you?"

"Yes." I stepped away from her and grabbed a chair from the dining table. I pulled it into the middle of the floor. "I want you to dance slowly for me, on me, around me. I want you to tie my wrists to the back of this chair. And then I want you to ride my dick, letting me come inside you as many times as I want until I'm satisfied." I took a seat, my large body covering the entire chair. My hard dick lay against my stomach, slightly tilted to the right. I stared at her and waited for her to make it happen.

"Very well." She walked into the other room and returned with black rope. She came up behind me and knotted my wrists against the wooden bars. The knot she made was so strong I couldn't slip out of it even if I used all my strength to break free.

She grabbed a remote, pointed it at her entertainment system, and hit a button.

Slow music came through the speakers, a wordless melody that would be perfect for a gentle sway. Most women would have been self-conscious with a request like that, but she got into the music immediately. She bent over and touched the top of her heels before she slowly pulled her fingertips back and up over her thigh. Her fingers continued to move up her body, past her tits, and all the way into her hair.

As if I weren't there, she danced.

She must have been familiar with this song because she knew every beat, every change in rhythm. She threw her hair back, rocked her hips, and popped her body at the right markers. Her eyes moved to mine without an ounce of uncertainty. She looked sexy—and she knew it.

I enjoyed the performance as my hands kept pulling on the rope. I'd asked her to tie me up, but now I wasn't so sure. I wished I could stroke my cock as I watched her, please myself before the grand finale.

God, I wanted her.

When the song came to an end, she walked over to me, taking her time as her heels hit the floor at every beat. She grabbed the back of my chair, leaned down, and kissed me on the mouth. It was soft but so sensual that I moaned. Her lips were soft and delicious, tasting like berry from her lipstick.

She stood back and pulled off her panties, letting them drop to the floor. Then she grabbed them, wrapped them around my length, and slowly jerked me as she straddled me.

I could feel her arousal all over me, mounds of it as she smeared it across my dick. She jerked me with the soft fabric, feeling almost as good as her pussy. She kissed me at the same time, giving me foreplay when I didn't need any more of it.

She pulled her panties off my dick and shoved them into my hands at the back of the chair.

My fingers immediately crumpled them, tucking them into a fist. "Take off your bra."

Her eyes narrowed in annoyance, knowing I wasn't the one who could make the commands. But she did it anyway, unclasping her bra and letting it fall.

I stared at her beautiful tits, loving their perkiness.

She had the sexiest nipples, hard and pink. "Fuck me slow."

She gripped the back of the chair as she guided herself down, taking in my length just as I asked. The slender muscles of her body worked to keep her balanced, to allow her to glide my cock and spread all of her arousal over me. She sat on my lap, her heels on the floor on either side of me.

I closed my eyes and clenched my jaw. I was never prepared for how amazing her pussy would feel. It always caught me by surprise. She was so tight, so wet. It was indescribable. "Fuck, Titan."

She breathed against my mouth as she allowed me to stretch her. "I love your cock, Hunt. It hurts like hell... but so good."

Our lips touched, but we didn't kiss. We just breathed together, our eyes on each other. When I looked at Titan, I didn't just see a gorgeous woman I wanted to fuck. I saw so much more now than I did before. I saw a woman who was strong and fearless. I saw a woman who was human just like I was, but she never let anyone realize it.

She wrapped her arms around my neck and used my muscular frame as an anchor to help her up and down my length. She took her time, clenching her thighs to hold her body. Then she slid back down, her slick pussy making a sexy sound every time she sheathed me to the balls.

My hands ached to grab her ass, squeeze her tits, anything. But I was restrained, unable to do anything but watch this woman fuck me in the sexiest way. She locked her eyes on me and watched my expression, her lips parted as she breathed deeply.

I loved watching her work to fuck me, watching her chest rise and fall with accelerated breaths to keep up with the pace. All the little muscles of her body flexed as they worked together to lift and lower her onto my length.

A hiss escaped her teeth. "I'm gonna come, Hunt."

"Come all over my dick, baby."

She moaned immediately, her pussy tightening around me.

I'd never called her baby, only Titan or Boss Lady. But the endearment came out anyway.

I moaned as I felt her grip me tightly, her body reacting before the orgasm even hit her. I'd fucked this pussy so many times that I knew it as well as I knew Titan herself. I knew when she was about to come before she even knew.

She rode me harder as she hit her orgasm, riding me until the climax had hit its peak and she came down again. Her sexy body was coated with a thin layer of sweat across her chest and her neck.

I wanted to lick it all away.

But now, my body was succumbing to her beautiful performance. My cock thickened and pulsed just before release. Then I pumped her full of all of my come, moaning as the spark of pleasure rocketed through me. "Fuck...I love your pussy."

She ground against me when I finished, her lips caressing mine. "She loves you too."

———

SHOWERING AFTER SEX HAD BECOME A NEW RITUAL FOR us. We were both so sweaty that it was necessary. I didn't want to sit on any of her expensive pieces of furniture and smear my bodily fluids all over them.

She probably felt the same way.

We always showered together, and it was one of the events I looked forward to. Of course, I loved watching warm water and soap run down a naked woman's body, but there was more to it than that. I loved the way her thoughts drifted away as she dug her hands into her hair and massaged her scalp. She was so comfortable with me she nearly forgot I was there.

Tatum Titan looked like a bombshell when her makeup was done. Paired with her clothes and heels, she turned heads everywhere she went. But I'd come to prefer this side of her, when she didn't have any makeup on at all.

She looked just like Tatum.

The woman, not the executive.

She smiled differently, in a genuine way that reached her eyes. She was a little playful, not all business and numbers. The skyscrapers she stacked around her came down noticeably. She showed more of herself to me.

I wondered if she trusted me.

She must have. Otherwise, she wouldn't partner with me.

"What?" She caught me staring at her.

"What?" I said back.

"You're staring at me."

"So?" She was mine. I could stare at her all I wanted.

She smiled then turned off the water. "Not much to see."

"I disagree."

She stepped out and dried off. I did the same. She had a large bathroom with two sinks, so I took one while she took the other. I dried my hair with the towel and examined my face in the mirror. I hadn't shaved in two days, and my hair was starting to get too thick. I knew

Titan liked my shadow. That was why I didn't shave it as often anymore.

"I'm having a get-together this weekend if you want to come."

I looked at her reflection in the bathroom mirror. "Having a party?"

"I wouldn't call it that." She patted her hair dry with the towel then turned on her hair dryer, the setting on low. Her fingers worked her strands of hair, looking sexy without even trying. A black silk robe was tied around her body, hiding her skin but not her curves. "It's just gonna be me and close friends."

That meant Thorn would be there.

Bastard.

"It'll be at my beach house in Rhode Island. I have a pool and a spa, and of course, the beach is right there."

So this would be a weekend party. It was a little too far to drive just for the day. I suspected she had a large mansion right on the sand, having all of her friends stay in bedrooms for the weekend. I shouldn't care that Thorn was going to be there since there was nothing to be jealous of. They weren't sleeping together now, and that was all that mattered.

But I didn't like him anyway. "What will I be attending this evening as?"

"Diesel Hunt, I suppose." She turned off the hair dryer and ran her fingers through her hair once again.

For such a sharp woman, she was dull sometimes. "Am I attending as your platonic friend and business partner? Or as your lover?"

"What does it matter?"

Oh, it mattered. I wasn't going to sit on the other side of the patio all weekend, watch her have fun with her friends in her bikini, and not walk up to her and kiss her whenever I wanted. "It does to me."

She peeled off her robe and hung it back on the hanger. She walked into her bedroom to pull on new clothes, and I followed her. She grabbed a fresh pair of panties from her drawer and pulled on an oversized t-shirt.

"Titan." When I didn't get an answer, I pressed harder.

"They all know about us, if that's what you're asking."

I already had to lie to my friends and my brother every single day. I didn't want to have to spend any extra time restraining myself. If I wanted to kiss her, goddammit, I was gonna kiss her. "Then I'd love to go."

"Great. I thought it would be fun to celebrate."

"I agree. We got a company with a lot of potential for a great price."

"And we fucked that asshole over." She smiled then walked into the living room. "You want anything to drink?" She didn't dismiss me right after sex the way she used to. Now it was another part of our routine to stay together, to watch a game or the nightly news. She even made dinner for me once.

"Water would be great."

She walked into her expansive kitchen, hidden from view. "Hungry?"

"I am if you're making something."

"I haven't eaten anything since lunch."

She didn't even eat lunch. She took a bite of her sandwich and ate some lettuce—that was it. "Me neither."

"Then I'll whip up something."

I felt awkward sitting there on the couch while she worked in the kitchen, so I walked in and joined her. She had just washed an assortment of vegetables and was now marinating shrimp. "Can I help you?"

"You don't need to worry about it, Hunt. I can handle it."

"I don't mind." I grabbed the wooden cutting board and found the chopping knife in one of the drawers. I started slicing the vegetables as she shook the bag of marinade. Once it was finished, she poured everything into the pan and started cooking.

I grabbed another pan for the veggies and took care of those. Standing side by side, we silently prepared a meal together.

I'd never done this before.

I prepared my own meals in solitude, or I had the maid take care of it before she left for the day. But I'd never cooked with a woman I was sleeping with. We usually went out to dinner then fucked before she left the next day.

I'd still hadn't gone out with Titan.

When the meal was prepared, we took a seat together at her kitchen table. Laid-back in a cotton t-shirt with hair still slightly damp, she looked soft as a peach. Her walls weren't up anymore, and she enjoyed the view of the city without a constant state of deflection.

She was a completely different person.

"Where should we start with the company?" She stabbed a spear of asparagus with her fork before she placed it into her mouth. "It's gonna take a lot of work. I know we both have our own holdings to manage, but we're gonna have to take a break and focus on this."

"I agree."

"We should make our offices in the building. Start the transition of power now."

"Agreed."

"Should we meet first thing in the morning every day?" she asked. "Over coffee?"

"How about we meet here instead?" I'd rather be naked with her than sipping coffee.

Her eyes narrowed in a pathetic attempt to look annoyed. If anything, she thought my comment was cute. "We have to establish a presence there. Our new employees need to see us, to feel reassured that the company isn't going under. Besides, we can screw on the desk. We'll make sure we don't get glass doors." She playfully rubbed her leg against mine under the table.

I'd thought I'd had my fill of her for the evening, but whenever she touched me, she lit me back up. "Sounds good to me. What did Thorn think about this partnership?" He must not have liked it. He wanted Titan all to himself. Now I was legally bound to her in a one way. It was just a single company, but it was something.

"He was hesitant at first, but he came around."

Their tight bond was obvious to me even when they weren't in the same room together. They spent time with his parents as a couple, and even though he didn't love her, he came all the way down to my office and claimed her. They told each other everything, when otherwise, Titan was committed to living a life of secrecy.

It annoyed me.

What did Thorn do to deserve her unflinching trust?

She'd already combined her life with his, agreeing to marry him for convenience rather than romance. I didn't consider myself to be a big romantic, but that sounded depressing. "How are you going to keep an arrangement with someone and be married to Thorn at the same time?"

She continued eating like the question didn't bother her. "I don't understand your meaning."

"You said you're monogamous with your partners. How will that work if you're married?"

"Thorn has his own lovers, so that won't be a problem. We'll do our separate things, just as we do now. It won't be that different."

Were they going to have separate bedrooms too? Having their partners over like roommates instead of husband and wife? "And will you ever have sex with each other?"

"Of course. There are times when we both aren't with other people."

I was annoyed anytime I saw Thorn wrap his arm around her waist. Imagining them screwing made me sick to my stomach. "What if the sex is bad?" If she'd never slept with him, how would she know?

"I doubt it." She placed another asparagus spear in her mouth, talking about sex with Thorn like it was the most normal thing in the world.

Underneath the skin, my blood was boiling. The veins in my forearms ached every time I clenched my fists. At what point in time did she think this was a good idea? I shouldn't worry about it because it wasn't like they were getting married tomorrow. Our relationship would end long before they took that step forward in their commitment. But it bothered me anyway. "And you're gonna have kids with him?"

"Yep." She finished her meal then placed her gaze on me. She examined my face like I was on the other side of her desk.

I knew that look.

"Why are you asking so many questions, Hunt?"

I did my best not to clench my jaw. "Sorry, I've never known anyone who's done an arranged marriage..." It was impossible to keep the annoyance out of my voice. I respected this woman, but I didn't respect her choice.

Titan straightened in her chair, her carefree attitude now abandoned. Even without wearing her dress and heels, she somehow looked as formidable as she did in the office. With wet hair and no makeup, she carried herself like a queen. "Hunt, I don't appreciate your judgments. You don't know me, so you don't know what's best for me."

"I know you enough to know you deserve the best."

She kept her rigidness, but her eyes softened. "Thorn is the best."

"If you think so, you need to take a harder look around." I wasn't suggesting myself, but I certainly was a better fit than he was. "How can you possibly think this is a good idea? What if you meet someone later and fall in love?"

"I won't."

"But what if you do?" I pressed.

She rested her chin on her fingertips, shifting her body to look directly at me. "Trust me, I won't." Her green eyes didn't shift as she stared me down. She seemed to be proving her point even more by not blinking.

I stared at her with the same intensity, a question burning in my mind. I knew this had something to do with her boyfriend who died. They were connected. There was no way they weren't. But Thorn warned me not to mention it to her. His savage reaction told me this subject was untouchable. I wanted to press and get my answers, but I didn't want to hurt her either. So I asked another question instead. "You don't believe in love?"

"I do—with all my heart."

I tilted my head, confused by her contradiction.

"I believe certain kinds of love exist. I believe my father loved me with everything he had. I loved him too.

I love my friends like family. They feel the same way. And I love Thorn as my best friend. Those are feelings that are undeniable. There's loyalty, trust, and friendship. But romantic love...I don't believe in that. I believe it's just misinterpreted passion and lust. The relationships aren't compatible because there's no foundation other than sex. And that's exactly why half of relationships end in divorce."

"What about relationships that are based on loyalty, trust, and friendship as well as lust and passion?"

Her eyes didn't move as they remained glued to mine.

"You don't believe in those?"

"I've never encountered a relationship like that."

I tried not to take the comment personally. She told me in the beginning what this relationship would entail. It's not like I wanted anything anyway, so I shouldn't care.

"Do you see yourself getting married?" she asked.

"I don't know."

"What about kids?"

"I don't know about that either." I'd never entertained the idea. I had yet to encounter a woman who wanted me for me, not my wealth or my bed. I was a mere security check for them. Sleeping with me was something they could brag about to their girlfriends. I was a trophy, an accomplishment they could set on their mantle.

"Well, I want a family. I want to hand off my legacy to someone when my time comes. In order to do that, I need a partner I can trust. With Thorn, we'll have a long and happy life together."

"You mean, a business arrangement." I was pressing her buttons, and I knew it. Instead of backing off, I kept going. If she were anyone else, I wouldn't care less. But I couldn't hold my tongue, not when I disagreed with her so strongly.

"Call it whatever you want." She grabbed her empty plate and walked back into the kitchen.

I knew I'd ruined a perfectly good night by not giving up. We probably would have sat on the couch together and watched the game, but instead, I chased her off. She felt innately comfortable with me, but now I'd botched that arrangement.

She came back into the dining room and took my plate. "You should get going, Hunt. I have to wake up early in the morning."

The blade came down and severed my head from my body. She dismissed me, finally fed up with my bullshit.

I could apologize and backpedal, but those would just be empty words. I wouldn't mean them, and she knew it.

She walked me to the door, her hands nowhere on me because she didn't want to touch me. She wore her cold and indifferent expression, closed off from me like an enemy rather than an ally.

I could just let this blow over, knowing it would get better in time. But I didn't want to do that. The elevator doors opened, but I didn't step inside. "You're right, I'm being judgmental."

She crossed her arms over her chest, the cotton t-shirt hugging her bare breasts. Her stony expression was slowly warming, softening back into the woman I'd come to know.

"Honestly...I'm not sure why it bothers me so much."

She shifted her weight to one leg, her bare foot flat against the floor.

"I guess I'm just protective of you." I'd never been that way with anyone else before. I always made sure the women who slept over had a ride home. I was there for Brett when he needed me. But I'd never dropped a net around someone like I did with Titan. I surrounded her on all sides, taking out anyone who crossed her. I walked away from a billion-dollar company just because the owner disrespected her. She'd proven herself completely capable, but I felt the need to look after her. But it was like a lion looking after a tiger—totally unnecessary.

Something in my words made her eyes soften like wilted rose petals. Her arms loosened around her body, and the affection in her gaze was undeniable. Her cold venom had been retracted, and now her beautiful calmness returned. "That's very sweet, Hunt. But I don't need anyone to be protective of me."

"Can't help it," I whispered. "I suspect that won't change. In fact, it'll probably get worse now that we're working together."

She smiled. "It's not so bad. I know I'll be protective of you too." She rose on her tiptoes, gripped my biceps, and kissed me on the cheek.

The touch was juvenile, like a young girl kissing a boy on a first date. But it was warm, her wet lips brushing against my skin. I loved the way she gripped my arms for balance as she raised herself up on her tiptoes.

"No one has ever been protective of me before," I whispered.

She rubbed her nose against mine. "There's a first time for everything, right?"

"Yeah...I guess you're right."

7

TITAN

ISA WALKED AROUND in her one-piece and heels. Her thick shades were over her eyes, and she sipped her margarita with a pink umbrella in the glass. "Where's your man at?"

"I don't know." I lounged on the armchair while the rest of my friends swam in the pool. We had a view of the beach, the waves gentle under the scorching sun. I was in a black two-piece, sunscreen rubbed into every single inch of my body, even my eyelids. "I'm sure he'll be here soon."

"Bringing any friends?" Isa asked.

"Better not be." If he wanted to be in my world, he had to learn to keep a secret.

Thorn walked out of the house in his black swim trunks. He had a plate of hamburger patties, and he carried it to the grill. His light-colored hair was flat on his head because he'd spent all day in the pool. Water dripped down his rock-hard body and fell to the concrete. "Who's hungry?"

"Me!" Everyone raised their hands.

"Who wants meat, and who wants processed garbage?" Thorn asked.

Pilar raised her hand. "Processed garbage for me, please."

"Me too." I didn't think black bean patties were garbage, but Thorn liked to blow his diet when he was on vacation—not that I disrespected him for it. He was all business when we were in New York, but when we traveled the world, he only wanted the finer things in life.

Thorn shook his head. "I expected more from you, Titan."

I pulled my shades down so I could look at him. "Then you don't know me very well."

"Is that a helicopter?" Pilar shielded her eyes as she looked up in the sky. She was sitting on a pink floaty in the pool. Her hair started to blow harder in the wind caused by the strength of the propellers. "It's landing right on your property, Titan."

I left my lounge chair and walked onto the pool deck. Sure enough, a black chopper was landing on the green grass adjacent to the house. I owned a lot of land because I wanted privacy away from everyone. The closest neighbor I had was ten miles away. I saw the logo on the side of the chopper.

Hunt Industries.

That could only be one person. "Looks like my man just arrived."

"In style," Pilar said. "He can fly a helicopter?"

"I want your leftovers when you're done with him," Isa said.

A jolt of jealousy shot through me, and I had no idea where it came from. I walked across the pool deck and to the stone pathway that led across the grass. The engine stopped, and the propellers came to a halt.

Hunt opened the door and stepped out. He was in jeans and a black t-shirt with aviator sunglasses on. He totally fit the part. "Mind if I park here?"

"Not at all."

He pulled off his helmet and placed it in the passenger seat. He walked toward me, grinning like a boy in love with his toy. When he got to me, he circled his arms around me and kissed me hard on the mouth, his fingertips digging into my skin. He lifted me off the ground, his muscular arms unflinching as he held me inches above the grass.

It was quite a kiss.

He pulled my bottom lip into his mouth before he set me back on my feet. "You've got a beautiful place."

"Thanks. You have a beautiful chopper."

"Thank you. I can give you a ride sometime if you'd like."

"If I'd like?" I asked. "I'd love that."

He grabbed his bag from the back seats and hooked it over his shoulder. He grabbed my hand with his, and he walked me back to the pool where everyone was watching us. Even Thorn stopped grilling the burgers just to look at us.

When Hunt walked by the pool, he raised his hand in the form of a wave. "Ladies."

"Hey, Hunt." Pilar waved, grinning wide.

Isa stared at his ass when he walked by, having no shame.

I bottled my jealousy for a second time.

Hunt walked up to Thorn, his smile disappearing within the snap of a finger.

Thorn did exactly the same.

It was tense, like two wild animals fighting for the same territory. They both looked each other in the eye, a quiet standoff between two alpha men. I didn't understand what the source of their conflict was. There was no reason for them to have beef with one another.

Thorn had encouraged me to pursue the relationship in the first place.

Hunt was the first one to extend his hand. "Burgers smell good."

Thorn shook his hand. "Want one?"

"Definitely." Hunt nodded before he walked into the house with me. "So, where are we staying?" He took a look around the large living room, seeing my white furniture and gray floors. It was decorated with a beach theme, a home away from home.

"This way." I took him down the hall to one of the big bedrooms. It had a private bathroom. It was a little bigger than all the others, but I knew Hunt was used to the finer things. He did show up in a helicopter, after all.

He set his bag down and took a quick look around.

"Is this okay?"

"Is this your room?"

"No. I'm in the master down the hall." The double doors were made of windows, and they opened up to the balcony overlooking the pool. It had a great view in the morning, when the waves were their calmest.

"With Thorn?" he asked.

"No." I guessed I should expect to get a lot of questions about Thorn from now on. "We don't sleep together."

"I thought I was hanging out this weekend as your lover."

I shut the bedroom door just in case anyone could overhear us. Everyone was outside enjoying the vibrant sunshine, but they could step inside to use the restroom. "You are."

"So don't you think we should stay in the same bedroom?" He moved his hands into his pockets, his cut arms looking muscular in his cotton shirt. It had a V neck, showing the muscular top of his chest. His sunglasses were still on the bridge of his nose, so I couldn't see his eyes.

"I don't sleep with anyone. I told you that."

"I think it's an appropriate time to make an exception." He never pressured me to do something I didn't want, but he was pushing this hard. "I don't want to fuck you then walk back down the hallway."

"My bedroom is right next door."

Hunt clenched his jaw before he pulled his sunglasses off his nose. He hooked them on to the front of his shirt, his dark eyes full of annoyance. He wasn't used to not getting his way—but he would never get his way with me. "I still think it's a waste of space."

"I don't care what you think," I said coldly. "This is how it is."

"Two weeks." He said it so quietly I could barely hear what he said.

"Sorry?"

"Two weeks until I'm in charge. And I promise you, everything will be different." He removed his watch and set it on the nightstand. "Let me change, and I'll join you outside."

I continued to stand in front of him stoically, but my heart was slamming inside my chest at a million miles an hour. I hadn't thought about the day everything would change, when Hunt would rule me for six weeks. I put it to the back of my mind because I didn't want to think about it. But it was approaching. It had seemed so far away, but now it was so near.

It was so close.

WE SAT AROUND THE FIRE PIT LATE INTO THE EVENING. We had leftover burgers from that afternoon, so everyone ate and roasted marshmallows over the fire. Hunt was in his swim trunks without a shirt, and my friends didn't hide their stares.

I couldn't blame them.

Hunt smeared the fresh marshmallow onto the

graham cracker with a piece of chocolate. "Want to split this with me?"

"Sure."

He picked it up and held it up to my mouth.

With my eyes locked on his, I took a small bite. I pulled back, a link of marshmallow goo stretching between my mouth and the rest of the s'more. It reminded me of the other night when Hunt's come had stuck from the head of his cock to my tongue. It stretched wider apart until it finally snapped in two.

Hunt watched my mouth, seeing my tongue swipe across my bottom lip to collect the white treat around my mouth. I had a stain of chocolate in the corner of my lips. His hand slid to the back of my head, and he leaned in to kiss me. His lips devoured the s'more off my mouth, and his kiss deepened as his tongue moved farther inside my body. It delved inside, exploring. The kiss became far too sexy for guests, but that didn't stop us. Hunt kissed me like he didn't give a damn who was watching.

He finally pulled away, his eyes on mine as he licked his lips.

Now I couldn't wait to go to bed.

I held up the rest of the s'more and fed him this time, placing it in his mouth until he took the entire piece. He chewed slowly as he stared at me, and once he got it down, he licked the chocolate off my fingertips.

"Jesus, I need a boyfriend," Pilar said as she excused herself and got another beer out of the ice chest.

Thorn had his arm around the model he'd brought up for the weekend, Milania. She didn't speak much English, but for the extent of their relationship, the language barrier wasn't an issue.

Hunt smirked at Pilar's words before he sucked the chocolate off his own fingers. "I'm gonna rinse off. I'll be back in fifteen minutes." He kissed me on the cheek just as I kissed him on the other before he got up. He walked back into the house, his ass unbelievably tight in his swim trunks.

When he was gone, Isa ran her mouth. "Jesus Christ, he's hot."

"I know," I said with a happy sigh. "What you saw just now is nothing."

Christy pouted her lips in pity. "I want a man like that. Every time I meet a guy, he ends up being a boy or a whore."

"Hey," Thorn said defensively. "Nothing wrong with being a whore."

"Hunt is a whore too," I reminded her. "He's not any different."

"I don't know about that," Isa said. "He seems to

like you."

"Because I'm sleeping with him," I reminded her. He was getting good sex from me on a regular basis. He'd better like me.

"I think it's more than that," Isa said. "Just the way he looks at you..."

"He does look at you very intently," Pilar said. "There was a pool full of hot chicks today, but he didn't even look at any of us."

"He's just discreet." He hid his wants and desires behind his eyes pretty well. When we first met, I couldn't read his expression at all. It seemed like he was mad all the time, actually.

"Whatever you say," Isa said.

The girls broke apart and jumped into the hot tub together, holding their beers as the jets frothed with bubbles. Milania joined them, leaving Thorn and me to sit together alone. We sat in silence for a while before I spoke.

"Milania is nice."

"She's alright." He spoke his mind whenever it was just the two of us, being completely transparent. When other people were around, he was always diplomatic. "Beautiful and experienced, but she talks too much."

"But she doesn't speak English."

"Which is why it's annoying."

I chuckled quietly so no one would overhear us.

"Is he staying until Sunday?"

"Yeah. Why?"

He shrugged.

Thorn didn't make eye contact with me, and his lack of intimacy was unusual. "Why do I get the impression you don't like him?"

"I never said that."

"Well, do you?"

He grinned. "No."

"Why don't you like him?"

"I just think he's an arrogant asshole, that's all."

"And you aren't?" I questioned.

He grinned again.

"Maybe you're too much alike."

"I just don't trust the guy."

"You trusted him weeks ago. You were the one encouraging me to be with him."

"But that was before…"

"Before what?" I pressed.

He took a long drink of his beer. "Nothing."

"Thorn." I was pulling teeth out of his mouth like a dentist. He resisted me the entire way.

"I think he has ulterior motives with you."

"What does that mean?" Thorn thought Hunt was trying to scam me? Every interaction I'd had with Hunt had been positive. He never gave me any reason to fear him. In fact, he proved how loyal he was in a world of crooks. "What kind of motives?"

"I don't think this is just an arrangement for him. I think he wants you to be his."

"As in, romantically?"

Thorn nodded.

I trusted everything Thorn said because he viewed the world with keen eyes. He had spectacular judgment. He'd become one of the most successful businessmen in the world because he was exceptional at what he did. "Why do you think that?"

"What Pilar said...the way he looks at you. The way he talks about you."

"When have you heard him talk about me?"

Thorn dodged the question. "The guy turned down a great offer because Bruce made some assholish remarks. Hunt could have made the deal and never told a soul what happened in that conference room. But he started a war—for you. Men don't go to war unless they're fighting for something they can't live without— like their woman."

"Hunt doesn't see me as his woman."

Thorn turned his face toward me, the fire highlighting his profile. "You so sure about that?"

"Yes."

"You need to think again, Titan."

I trusted Thorn with my life. I should trust him about this too. "I'll ask him about it."

He looked back into the fire, watching it dance with his crystal blue eyes. "And in the event that my suspicion is right...what will you say?"

"What do you mean?"

He rubbed his palms together, staring at his hands as they glided past each other. "Is this more than an arrangement to you? As your future husband, I'd like to know if our commitment to one another has changed."

Now that I knew the source of Thorn's unease, I smiled. "Are you jealous, Thorn Cutler?"

He smiled back and shrugged. "I'm more concerned than jealous. We made this arrangement a long time ago. Things change..."

"Nothing has changed, Thorn. I like Hunt a lot... I love everything about him. I admit I feel differently about him than I did the others before him. I'm actually happy that I'll still get to see him once this arrangement is over. I want him to be in my life... I want him to be my friend. But no, there's nothing more than that there."

Thorn nodded. "That was the reassurance I wanted. But you should still talk to him...make sure you're on the same page."

While Hunt said and did sweet things, I didn't think

his affection was deeper than that. But it didn't hurt to ask. It wouldn't be the first time I was wrong about something.

———

I DUG MY FINGERS INTO HIS HAIR AS WE MOVED TOGETHER on the bed. He was buried deep inside me, holding his muscular body on top of mine. My ankles were locked around his waist, and unlike when we were at home, we both did our best to stay quiet.

Mostly so we didn't make everyone jealous of the hot sex we were having.

I'd made him fuck me for nearly thirty minutes straight, subjecting him to watching me come over and over. Every time he looked like he was about to explode, I slapped him across the face. That halted him in the moment, but it also made him burn even hotter.

I was just about to come for the third time, and this orgasm somehow felt stronger than the previous two. My fingers dragged down his skull to his muscular back, feeling the individual muscles shift as he arched his back then thrust his hips, digging deeper into me. His hard jaw was etched in a sexy scowl, anxious to fill me with all the come he was desperate to release. "I'm about to come..."

He ground against me harder, his balls smacking against my ass. "I know, baby."

My nails skimmed down his back to his ass, and I gripped the powerful muscle tightly. "Come with me."

He growled against my mouth, his body shaking in relief now that he had my permission.

"Almost there..." I breathed into his mouth, our lips brushing against one another, exchanging kisses and heated breaths. I closed my eyes when I felt everything down below tighten. I gripped his cock like a fireman squeezed his hose. "Fuck...here it comes."

His final pumps were hard, smacking the headboard into the wall. He took a deep breath and held it just before he came. Then an angry moan escaped his lips, the vein in his forehead bulging as he found his release. He filled my drenched pussy with all of his come, and when he was finished, he still thrust gently inside me, the products of our arousal still moving together. "Damn..."

I ran my hands through his hair and kissed him, giving him tender embraces with lots of tongue. He pleased me so well, made me come harder than any other man before him. "That was good..."

"You make me good, Boss Lady."

"Making a woman come so many times is no easy feat...you know what you're doing."

"I'm glad I get to use all my experience on you." He kissed me a few more times before he pulled out of me, his soft cock still impressive.

I loved sleeping when I was still full of him, still connected to him in some way.

He rolled over and lay beside me, his glistening pecs solid. His chest rose and fell slowly, and he placed one arm behind his head. He stared at the ceiling, his hair a complete mess from my fingers.

I turned over and ran my fingers up his body, tracing the hard abdominals just above his hips. I felt each groove, thinking of rocks along a riverbed. His tanned skin was beautiful, flawless. His muscles stretched the skin in all the right places. He filled out his clothes perfectly, and he looked even better naked.

I hooked my arm around his waist and rested my face on his shoulder, smelling both of our scents mixed together. It was vanilla, sweat, and his cologne all wrapped up into one—good sex.

He rested his arm on mine and turned his face slightly toward me. "Can you feel me inside you?"

"Yes."

His moan was so quiet I could barely hear it.

"Does that turn you on?"

He answered instantly. "Yes."

"It's one of my kinks too."

"I've never fucked a woman without a condom, so this is a first for me."

Several thoughts flashed through my mind when I heard what he said. I'd never asked him about his past love life. I hadn't cared about the women before me or those who would take my place once I was gone. But now I felt a warm sensation between my legs—and not because of his seed. "Not once?"

"No."

"Not when you lost your virginity?"

"No."

I propped myself up on my arm and looked down at him. "I'm surprised."

"It's not that surprising." He looked at me as his fingers moved through my hair. "A lot of women would love to get knocked up by me, force me to be stuck with them. It'd be a great way to access my wealth. So I never trust a woman, even if she says she's on the pill."

"Then why did you trust me?"

"Because you're Tatum Titan." His fingers moved along my neck. "You don't need me for anything."

I looked into his dark gaze and thought about warm coffee on a winter day. I loved the way they lightened when he was outside in direct sun. They carried the color of hazelnut, a brighter color that made him look soft. In the dark or when he was moody, they took on the color of coffee beans—dark and textured. "What do you think of it?"

"Baby, there's nothing like it."

I'd noticed he'd started calling me baby often. I hated nicknames because they were sexist and annoying. But that endearment fell nicely on my ears. It made me feel cherished, desired. If someone else would have said it, I would have told him to knock it off. But I never told Hunt to stop.

The thoughts brought me back to what Thorn said to me. "There's something I want to ask you."

"Go for it."

"We're honest with each other, so I know you'll tell me the truth."

He smiled before he sat up, propping himself on one arm the way I was. He pivoted his body toward me. "This should be good."

"Thorn thinks you see this as more than just an arrangement...that you see me as something more than a temporary partner."

His expression didn't change at all. His eyes were the identical mocha color, and a slight smile was still plastered across his lips. With the same confidence he took into the office every day, he held my gaze. "And what do you think, Titan?"

I tilted my head at the question, surprised he

answered my question with a question. "What does it matter?"

"Because I want to know if you're really the one asking. If this something you're concerned about. Or is this something he's concerned about. Who am I talking to right now?"

Those simple words told me he disliked Thorn as much as Thorn disliked him. The two men in my life didn't care for one another—even despised each other. Thorn had never had a problem with the other men I took to bed. And I never disliked any of his girls, even if they were a little annoying at times. "You're talking to me...but he's the one who brought it up."

"He seems jealous."

"He's not."

"We both know he doesn't like me."

Hunt was a lot more observant than I gave him credit for. He handled himself so well around Thorn that I couldn't help but respect him even more. "He's just a little paranoid."

"Paranoid about what?"

The answer was complicated, but since Hunt knew all the backstory, it would make sense to him. "That you're going to take me away from him."

"If he's that concerned about it, maybe he should give you more. Treat you better."

"I don't want to be in a relationship him. I love him to the end of the earth and back...but I don't see him that way."

"Maybe he sees you that way." He still maintained the same expression even though he'd managed to turn the tables on me and make me question Thorn when I was supposed to be questioning him. "But he knows you don't feel the same way."

"I don't know...doesn't seem that way."

Hunt finally turned his gaze away. "Something to think about."

WE PACKED ALL OF OUR THINGS AND PREPARED TO LEAVE my home in Rhode Island. Thorn's driver was going to return both of us to New York, while everyone else took their own vehicles.

And Hunt took his chopper.

"How about I give you a lift home?" Hunt asked as he pulled his bag over his shoulder.

"In the helicopter?" I asked in surprise.

"Yeah. The flight is only thirty minutes."

"It's not the duration I'm worried about."

"Come on, it's beautiful. Unless you don't trust me?"

I trusted this man more than a commercial pilot. He would get us there safely. "My luggage?"

"It'll fit."

I couldn't suppress my smile at the thought of being that high in the sky, flying over the coast back into the city. I'd be able to see the skyscrapers long before I was even close to them. Flying had always been exhilarating for me. Some people were terrified of being in the air and preferred their feet planted against the earth, but I was the opposite.

I preferred the sky.

"Sounds like fun."

Hunt showed his enthusiasm by pulling me in for a hard kiss on the mouth. He gripped my blouse at the small of my back, bunching up the fabric as he breathed hard into my mouth. When he pulled away, he wore a handsome smile. "Then let's prepare for takeoff."

We said goodbye to everyone, and the maids were already taking care of the mess we left behind. Thorn didn't look too pleased about me jumping into a heli-copter, but he didn't question me in front of everyone.

After securing our luggage in the back, we pulled on our helmets, and Hunt spoke to someone over his head-set. He issues some codes before he gripped the gear and lifted the helicopter into the air.

"Oh my god." I clutched at the door as I peered

down to see my house, which was getting smaller and smaller. "My house looks so tiny."

With aviator sunglasses and a thick helmet, he looked sexy as hell. The sun was bright on his face, and he looked like a man who still possessed the spirit of a boy. He was a pilot, taking a beautiful piece of machinery into the sky.

I watched him with a smile on my face, loving seeing Hunt so excited.

It was difficult to tell where he was looking with those glasses, but he must have been looking at me because he said, "What?"

"What?" I repeated.

"Why are you staring at me?"

"Because you're cute."

"Cute?" he asked, his eyebrows furrowing. "I'm a man, and men aren't cute."

"Fine. You look sexy."

He directed the helicopter northwest. "That's better."

"So...have you ever gotten a blow job while flying?"

"Not while piloting," he said. "And as much as I would like one now, I'll have to turn down your offer."

"Why?"

"Too dangerous."

"Safety man. I like it."

We flew most of the way in silence, taking in the

spectacular views under the clouds. The rotors were so loud that we could only speak to each other through the intercom system in our headsets. It was a strange way to talk, but I got used to it after the first few sentences.

When we arrived in New York City, it was an even bigger treat. The sun was starting to set, and the lights looked so beautiful. It wasn't much different from the view out the windows of my penthouse, but at this height, the city actually seemed small. "Most beautiful thing I've ever seen."

He turned his head my way. "Yeah."

"I moved here when I was fifteen." I remembered the day my dad relocated after he was let go at his job. "I was raised in a small town in New Jersey. My dad was a painter, and when he lost work, he had to move here to find something else. Money was always a challenge because he had to keep finding work. When he worked for a bigger business, he never made enough money." I didn't know why I was telling him any of this. It was personal and boring, but my mouth kept moving. "When I was old enough to start working, I helped out. It made everything a lot easier on my dad. But then he got sick...and there's wasn't anything I could do." When I thought about the final six months of my father's life, I was full of heartbreak. But I tried not to think about it too deeply. If I did, I'd start to cry. "I wanted to be rich because I wanted to take care of my father. He took care of me when my mother proved how easy it was to just run off. He stuck by my side and gave me the best life he could. I wish he could see me now...to see what I've done."

"Who says he doesn't see you right now?"

I turned my head his way and saw the affectionate look in his eyes. His sunglasses were gone, revealing his expression for me to see. His smile was encouraging, but his eyes held heartbroken understanding.

"I'm sure he's proud of you, Titan. I just met you a few months ago, and I'm proud of you."

"Yeah?" I whispered.

"If I ever have a daughter, I hope she's just like you."

"Why?"

"You don't take shit from anyone—and that's how I'd want her to be. She would know her value—just the way you know yours. She wouldn't be afraid to kick a man in the balls if he touched her the wrong way. If someone disrespected her, she would make him pay for his foolishness."

No one ever praised me the way Hunt did. Most people just cared about how I started my business, where I learned all my secrets. They wanted to take my playbook and use it to their advantage. Hunt was the first person to compliment my character, not my success.

It was a nice change. "I don't think anyone has ever said anything so nice to me."

"I kinda like you. I don't do business with anyone, so I guess that was obvious."

"I like you too, Hunt."

"You want your son to be like me?" he teased.

I didn't think much about my kids or how they would be. All I knew was that I wanted them. But when I pictured Hunt as a little boy, it made me smile. He must have been adorable. "Wouldn't be the worst thing in the world."

BRETT MAXWELL CALLED ME WHILE I WAS AT THE OFFICE.

"Hey, Brett," I said as I typed an email at the same time. "How are you?"

"I'm great. I was hoping I could swing by in a few minutes. I've got the final commercial edited."

I didn't care that much about it. I could just watch it on TV whenever it aired. But since he was excited about it, I went for it. "Sure. I'll tell Jessica you're coming."

"See you then."

Just when I hung up, Hunt called me.

"Hello, Mr. Hunt," I said in a snooty business voice. "How can I help my partner today?"

"You could start by talking to me like that while I fuck you."

He always started with the vulgar comments right off the bat. "Doesn't sound so bad. I wish I'd gotten different doors now…" I'd order him down here on my lunch break if I could. He'd fuck me good on my desk, and then leave immediately afterward. His come would stay buried inside me until I got home and took a shower.

"You know, there are people you can hire to take care of that for you."

"I don't want to make it obvious."

"Since when did Tatum Titan start caring about what her four assistants thought?" he questioned. "I can come down there and change those doors for you right now."

"In tight jeans with a tool belt?"

"Whatever you want, baby."

"And without a shirt?"

"Of course."

"Hmm…sounds nice."

"And you know what? I'll do it for free."

"I was hoping you'd want some other compensation for it…"

His voice was silent, but I could feel his heavy breathing through the phone. He was probably gripping a pen right now, a raging hard-on in his slacks. "You're lucky your two weeks aren't up yet..."

"Why?" I was playing a dirty game. I rolled the dice, not caring whether I won or lost. "What would you do right now if you were calling the shots?"

Another pregnant pause of silence. He was probably clenching his jaw right now, grinding his teeth together. "There's a Four Seasons across the street from my building. I'd book a room, have you meet me there, and then I would throw you on the bed with your ass over the edge. I'd eat your pussy, finger your ass, shove my cock down your throat, and then I'd fuck you in the ass until you couldn't take it anymore. I would come inside you twice, pumping you with so much of my seed that you could barely hold on to it. Then I'd order you to go back to work and keep it in there...until later tonight when I'd order you to show it to me. Titan, if I were in charge, that's what we'd be doing right now."

Now I was the one rendered speechless, my voice gone and only my shaky breath remaining. All my confidence evaporated once his dominion had crushed mine. He still had two weeks until his regime could begin, but he'd obviously been planning every single moment of it. "I...I've gotta go."

"Alright, baby." His grin was loud through the phone. "Hope you don't miss me too much today."

Damn, I already missed him right now.

I hung up just when Brett was ushered into my office by Jessica. I cleared my throat and tried to keep the flushed color out of my cheeks. But when I looked at Brett, a man similar to Hunt in so many ways, it was difficult to clear the fog that thickened in my mind. His eyes were identical to his brother's, and they had the exact same intensity. "Hey, Brett. It's great to see you again." I came around the desk and shook his hand.

"The pleasure is all mine, Titan." He pulled the satchel off his shoulder and pulled out a sleek gray laptop. "How are things going?"

They'd been better. My hand would be in between my legs right now if I had enough privacy. "Good. You?"'

"I've very happy with the way the commercial turned out. You and Hunt look like you belong together."

My heart leapt into my throat.

Brett didn't see my reaction because he was opening the file on his computer. He moved a few things around before he opened it to full screen. Music projected from the speakers, accompanied by the sound of powerful motors running. And then there was me, driving down the windy road with Hunt right behind me. Scenes cut and shifted, going back and forth between us. Hunt smiled at my competitiveness, appreciating the challenge. I didn't look challenged at all. After a few more cuts, the commercial ended and brought up a black screen of current auto deals.

Looking at Hunt didn't help.

"What'd you think?" Brett shut the laptop.

"It was phenomenal. People will love it."

He smiled at the compliment. "That's what I'm hoping for. I intend to sell a lot more cars this year. Photographers have snapped Hunt in his Bullet around town a lot, and my numbers have spiked ever since. But let's see how they spike when you're the one being featured."

I hoped there was a spike at all. Not a lot of men respected my success, thinking my vagina was some kind of handicap. "We'll see."

"I'm having lunch with Hunt today, so I'll show him then."

Was I the only one who thought it weird for him to call his brother by a last name different from his own? "Thanks for stopping by. I appreciate it."

"Anything for you, Titan. My brother told me you just acquired Bruce's company—congratulations."

"Thank you." We had our work cut out for us, but we'd make it work. With the kind of discipline between us, we would make things move at a rapid pace.

"My brother is very picky when it comes to business.

He obviously has a great deal of respect for you."

When Brett's eyes drilled into my face just the way Hunt's did, I walked around the desk and put space between us. "And I him. He's a brilliant man."

"I don't know about brilliant," he said with a chuckle. "But he's got a good head on his shoulders." He slipped the laptop back into the case and took a seat in the armchair. "And he's not as arrogant as he could be, I suppose."

He was cocky sometimes, but only in good ways.

"My brother is exceptionally fond of you. Never has anything but nice things to say about you. Since he doesn't say much at all, it's a pretty big deal."

It seemed like he was trying to fish something out of me. "I consider us to be good friends."

"I bet that would be different if Thorn weren't around."

My heart froze.

"He's never said anything to me, but I'm his older brother. I can read him better than he realizes. He'd be ticked at me if he knew I said anything to you, but since he's always ticked at me, doesn't make much of a difference." He rested his fingers against the side of his head, smiling.

"He's been nothing but professional toward me." When Hunt said his brother was onto us, I didn't realize how serious he was. Maybe he did know, and he was just trying to get a confession out of one of us. "Men and women can just be friends. I see it all the time. A man like Hunt has his pick of any woman he wants. A workaholic like me isn't exactly desirable."

"I highly doubt that." He still wore his endearing smile. "I knew there was something more there at the racetrack—and at the shoot."

What happened at those two places? We'd been distant with each other in the public eye. Hunt had come to my room a few times, but no one ever caught us. "Why?"

"Watching you drive like that nearly gave him a heart attack. He wouldn't feel that way for just anyone."

I still didn't understand the significance. "Why?"

"Because that's how our mom died."

My heart stopped beating, and sorrow like I'd never know seeped into my veins. I'd lost my father tragically, and he lost his mother in a terrifying way. I knew his mother had passed away, but I had no idea how.

"Some kids were speed racing on a deserted road, ran a stop sign, and killed her on impact."

God, Hunt.

"I could tell he was genuinely afraid for you. I'd never seen him like that. You're obviously very special to him—whether he'll tell you that or not."

8

HUNT

My PI walked inside right before lunch. Tom Hutch was one of the best detectives in the city. He could dig up info that happened before technology was even around. You could ask about something that occurred in the sixties, and he would track it down.

He placed the manila folder on my desk. "Got everything you asked for."

Sitting on my desk was everything about Titan's boyfriend—the one who died. I'd asked Tom for every piece of evidence surrounding that case. I wanted to know everything about their relationship prior to that event. Was there talk of marriage? What happened after he died? Had Titan not had a boyfriend ever since?

"I found a lot more than I expected. There's a few other police reports you'll find interesting."

Police reports?

"I think this case wasn't solved correctly. They never caught the killer—but I think it's obvious who did it."

I stared at the folder. Heartbeats passed, and all I did was blink.

"Do you need anything else, sir?"

I finally came back to attention, looking at the man sitting across from me. "That'll be all, Tom. Thank you."

"My office will bill you." He walked out, leaving me alone in my office.

Everything I wanted to know was sitting right in front of me. I could understand Titan better, understand the woman who was slowly becoming my obsession. I wasn't just fascinated by the powerful woman I was fucking. I wanted to know the other woman that I met briefly but never got to know.

I wanted to know Tatum.

Thorn warned me not to ask her about it. Said he would kill me if I did. The threat didn't bother me, but the passion behind it affected me. He'd turned protective like a watchdog, defending the woman he intended to spend his life with.

I respected that.

I grabbed the folder and pulled it toward me, but I didn't open the cover. It was thick with paper, probably filled with police reports and photos. This wasn't a simple case if this much information was included in the file.

I grabbed the bottom corner and prepared to open it.

But I knew it was wrong.

I was snooping around behind her back.

I was sticking my nose where it didn't belong.

I was invading her privacy.

She had the right to tell me if she wanted me to know. Paying someone a fortune to pay off cops and lawyers to get this information was morally wrong.

I despised myself for even getting this far.

I opened the bottom drawer of my desk, dropped the folder inside, and slammed it closed.

I respected her with every fiber of my being. I couldn't do that to her.

I couldn't betray her.

I didn't believe in love. But I certainly believed in loyalty.

And my loyalty to her was unbreakable.

"WOULD YOU LIKE SOME WINE?" TITAN WALKED OUT OF the kitchen with two glasses of red wine.

"Yes. Thank you." She set the glass in front of me,

but instead of sitting in the other chair at the dining table, she slid onto my lap. She straddled me, her fingers cupping the bottom of the bulb of the glass.

Her dress rose to her hips as she lowered herself, her black panties visible.

My hands gripped her thighs, and I rocked my hips gently, my cock anxious to see her. I'd never been offered refreshments when I first came over. We seemed to get right down to business, fucking hard on every piece of furniture in the house.

This was a change of pace.

She sipped her wine as she stared at me, her long lashes thick with mascara. When she pulled the glass away, her lipstick was smeared across the area where her mouth had been just a second ago.

I didn't know if this was leading somewhere, but it was perfectly okay if it wasn't. Just holding eye contact with her was an erotic experience. A woman could never challenge my gaze with the same confidence she possessed. She had so much power, and she wasn't afraid to use it.

She set her glass down before she unbuttoned my collared white shirt, making my bare chest visible for her enjoyment. She pushed the shirt back toward my shoulders then slid my tie out of the collar.

She grabbed her glass next, and then purposely spilled it down my chest.

It was an $800 shirt, but who gave a damn. This woman could do whatever she wanted to me.

She leaned down and licked the wine away, absorbing the drops on her tongue. She slid to the floor to get the liquid that had reached my boxers. She even pulled back the band so she could stick her tongue down my crotch.

And lick my dick.

She came back up and straddled me again, acting so sexy with so much confidence.

I'd never seen anything like it.

She massaged my shoulders next, her eyes on me once more. She examined my eyes then explored the rest of my face. Her look lingered on my chin, the coarse hair that had come in since that morning, and she examined my lips, the ones that kissed her every single day. She cupped my cheek and ran her slender fingers along my jawline.

I felt like a muse.

Her fingers slid over the jut of my jaw and then down my neck until she reached my chest again.

During moments like these, I enjoyed our quiet conversations. I enjoyed getting to know her, taking what little she would give me. But right now, she seemed to be in a unique mood. She wasn't fucking me, but she was enjoying me in a different way. "Have you enjoyed being with me?"

My eyes opened wider at the question, expecting her to say nothing rather than that. "The answer is obvious."

"Then let's keep it this way for another six weeks—no switching."

She was asking me to give up my domination. She wanted to remain in charge, be the alpha even longer.

Not gonna happen. "No."

Her fingers slid down my chest, her face exactly the same as it was before.

"I've enjoyed fucking you the way you ask. I've enjoyed fulfilling your fantasies. I've enjoyed this arrangement a lot more than I thought I would. So I have no doubt in my mind you're going to enjoy every second of my reign."

"We're different people..."

"Doesn't matter. I know I've earned your trust. You trust me as much as Thorn. You wouldn't own a business with me if you felt otherwise."

"Business is different than sex."

"We both know that's not true—they're exactly the same."

She held my gaze with waning confidence.

"There's no reason to be scared, baby. You won't want me to stop. That's a promise."

"I have control issues..."

My hands slid to hers, and I interlocked our fingers tightly. I squeezed her as I held her gaze steady. "Do you trust me, Titan?"

She stared at me for long moments. Time seemed to slow down because the intensity of our gazes was sucking the life out of both of us. My fingers continued to caress hers, comforting her in her elegant distress. Her eyes shifted slightly, back and forth as they looked into mine. "Yes..."

I brought both of her hands to my lips and kissed each knuckle, worshiping her with my mouth. This woman gave me a shot of adrenaline that jumping out of a plane wouldn't match. She gave me control even when I was the one tied to a chair. She gave me scorching intimacy, a new level of erotic sex that I didn't know existed.

She gave me so much.

"And I trust you."

Titan and I didn't waste any time turning Carol's business inside out. We called for a remodel of all the lobbies and the hallways. We each had a distinct vision for our business, and while they were slightly different, elegance was important to both of us.

So we agreed on a lot of things.

Both of our offices were located on the top level, on opposite ends of the floor. We each had a spectacular view of Manhattan, both of our offices the exact same size. The floors were being replaced, the windows were being cleaned, and a new coat of paint had been added to the walls. Titan had a few specific changes she wanted, and I suspected I knew exactly how her space would look. She had a particular style.

But since both of our spaces were under construction, we shared a conference room with a large window. A solid door and walls separated us from the assistants that were now under our regime. I hadn't fucked her during working hours yet, but that was because I'd been too focused on getting shit done. I still had other businesses to manage, an entire empire that required my full attention.

She had a white laptop with brightly colored stationery. Everything she owned was distinctly feminine, matching her undeniable sex appeal. She rocked bright red lipstick like it was her natural shade, and pencil skirts fit her so well they were a second skin.

She was definitely distracting.

I'd had beautiful employees working for me all my

life, but I'd never been tempted by their appearance. Somehow, I separated them into a different category, knowing business and pleasure didn't mix.

But I wouldn't have had that same strength if Titan were my assistant.

But then again, a woman like her would never work for someone else. That was why I was attracted to her in the first place.

Because, you know, she had great tits.

"Yes?" Titan's eyes burned into mine as she stared at me across the table, a white pen in her hand.

I didn't realize I'd been staring at her. "Nothing."

"You stared at me for five minutes."

I smiled before I focused my attention on my screen. "I was thinking about your tits...as I often do during the day."

"As flattered as I am, we need to remain professional when we're here. We're business partners, and we can't afford to mix business and pleasure while we're here. Not just now, but for the future."

Because we wouldn't always be fucking. She'd be married to Thorn with a couple of kids at home. There'd be another boy toy waiting for her at the penthouse when she got off work. "Can't make any promises."

"Then I'll keep the promise for both of us."

Until I was in charge. I shut my laptop and set my pen down on my notepad. My ankle rested on the opposite knee, and I stared at her, my hands lying together on my lap.

She finished typing her sentence before she met my look, her green eyes lustrous with her heavy makeup meticulously done. "Yes?"

"I've enjoyed the things we've done together, but I was under the impression things would get more serious."

Her eyes shifted slightly, looking deep into my gaze like there was more to see. "What do you mean by that, Hunt?"

"I thought you would take it to another level. I thought there would be whips and chains by now."

"Who said there won't be?"

The corner of my lip tugged into a smile. "I haven't seen anything yet."

"I was too busy enjoying you. Didn't think about it."

"So I'm enough for you?"

She dropped her gaze and turned back to her computer. "I guess you could put it that way. We have a strong chemistry. It's been enough up until this point."

I expected her to whip me until I bled, to chain me down and pour hot wax all over me. I'd never been into that, but I enjoyed Titan so much that I wondered if I would enjoy it. I'd adored everything else about her. And more importantly, I trusted her to bring me to oblivion.

"Hunt, are you telling me you want to do those things?"

I shrugged in response. "I'm open to it—that's all I'm saying."

A confident smile stretched over her lips. "You take submission well."

"Not as well as you're about to."

Her smile disappeared immediately. No matter how powerful our connection was, she would always show her hesitance at the exchange of power. I didn't know why it was so difficult for her, especially when I did it so well. She was about to kneel before me, but submitting to me would be the most freeing experience of her life.

I opened my laptop again, unable to hide the smirk on my face. I only had eight days to go before she was exclusively mine. I would be the only man in the world who got to enjoy Tatum Titan this way. I was going to conquer her harder than a dictator dominated a new land. "Use your remaining time wisely."

———

"Brett Maxwell is here to see you, sir."

I had a meeting in fifteen minutes, but I always had time for my brother. "Send him in."

Brett walked through the door a moment later, in dark jeans and a sports jacket. "Busy?"

"You know I'm always busy. What's up?" I sat back in my chair and interlocked my fingers.

"Are you still going to put in that offer on Megaland?"

Megaland was a technology company that designed some of the greatest innovations in our lifetime. They had the best researchers, the most brilliant minds, and the soundest strategy. Problem was, they were a small company. They didn't have the budget to progress, to hire more creators to increase their productivity. They were constantly being beaten out by large corporations, but not because their products were inferior; they simply couldn't market themselves on the same level.

That's where I came in.

"Yes."

Brett sighed before he sat down, his shoulders rigid like he had bad news.

"What's the problem, Brett?"

"You aren't gonna like it..."

"I can handle it. Spit it out." I leaned back in my chair and propped the side of my face on my hand.

"I heard through my sources that your father is currently in the process of making an offer."

I wore the same stoic expression, appearing as cold as stone on a winter day. My father and I hadn't spoken in five years. An unspoken war had started between us. When I started my own business and turned my back on his company, he considered it to be a stab in the back. He'd never forgiven me for it.

And I'd never forgive him for what he did to Brett.

I wondered if Vincent Hunt had caught wind of my plans and wanted to go head-to-head with me. It could just be a coincidence, but with men like my father, there was no such thing as coincidence. I passed him on the Forbes list a year ago, and that must have left an acidic taste in the back of his mouth.

Brett watched me as he waited for me to say something. "Hunt?"

I snapped out of it. "How credible is your source?"

"Pretty damn credible."

"What makes you so sure?"

"Because he's one of the three guys who owns Megaland. He bought a car from me last week."

Fuck. Then it was true.

"If you're gonna take this company, you need to do it now."

"Do you know anything about the offer itself?"

"No," Brett said. "But when Vincent learns you're his competitor, he'll do anything to outbid you—even if it's a terrible deal."

He was a proud motherfucker. "Shit."

"Yeah..." He rubbed his chin as he looked out the window, his eyes identical to mine.

"What did you think of the guy who bought the car from you?"

"Nerdy smart," he answered. "You know, a tech genius from Silicon Valley with no people skills. You know the type."

That didn't surprise me.

"But a nice guy. Said he wants a nice car so chicks knew he had money." He chuckled quietly. "If you've got game, you don't need to prove you have money. But I didn't tell him that. He's young and needs to learn."

At least now I had a picture of what my client looked like. "Thanks for passing this along to me, Brett."

"No problem. What are big brothers for?"

"Cars, apparently." I told an easy joke to lighten the mood, but I was too bleak inside to laugh at my comment.

He chuckled then rose out of his chair. "How's Titan doing?"

Paranoid settled on my shoulders. "How would I know?"

He buttoned the front of his jacket. "Don't you work with her every day now?"

That was it. I did. "We don't talk much..."

"You're reinventing a company together, but you don't interact?" he asked incredulously. "Uh, good luck." He gave me a quick wave before he walked out.

Once the door was shut and I was alone, all I could think about was the situation I was in. In order to avoid any interaction with my father, I could just back off and let him take Megaland. But I knew if this were anyone else, even Titan, I wouldn't back down. This company was a gold mine, and I wasn't going to let someone take it from me.

I WORKED FROM HOME THAT NIGHT, DRINKING RED WINE at the table while my empty plate was pressed to the side. My housekeeper made me vegetarian meatloaf for dinner, knowing I was very selective with my diet. Low fat and high protein was the only diet that could sustain my physique. At the age of thirty-five, I wasn't exactly young anymore. I had to work out twice as hard and eat even less if I wanted to look like this.

And since I landed women like Tatum Titan, it was totally worth it.

Titan texted me. My phone was sitting on the table, and it lit up once the words were on the screen. I didn't even realize how dark it was in my penthouse because I'd been focused on what I was doing, not the sun disappearing behind the skyscrapers. *Come over.*

It was the one occasion where I didn't want to see her. I was on a serious deadline and didn't have time to fuck around tonight. *I can't tonight.*

I think otherwise.

I liked her hard edge, but right now, I didn't need it. *I can't tonight, Titan. Tomorrow.* I set my phone aside and got back to work. I needed to know everything about these guys before I walked into their tiny office and made my offer. I knew I was a dream investor, but honestly, so was my father. If they figured out we were related, then they would know they could have a serious bidding war on their hands. And since this wasn't about money, they could easily take advantage of the situation. It was complicated, to say the least.

Titan called me.

Her name appeared on the screen, exuding power in just the simple word.

I answered. "Yes?" I didn't bite back my irritation. Being told what to do was fun any other time, but not now.

"Everything alright?" Instead of the sexy, bossy tone

I was used to hearing from Titan, I got to hear the soft concern from Tatum—the woman I'd only just met.

"I've got a lot on my plate right now…"

"For work?"

"Yeah." I didn't want to bore her with the details, but I also wanted to talk about it. She opened up to me. Maybe she wanted me to open up to her. "My father and I are competing for the same company. I've got to get my offer in by tomorrow. I'll be working all night."

After a long pause, she spoke. "Can I help?"

She was one of the busiest people in the world. She told me she hardly slept at night, constantly working around the clock. It surprised me she would make an offer like that. She wasn't the kind of person to make such an offer unless she really meant it. "Don't worry about it. I can handle it."

"I really don't mind, Hunt. Two heads are better than one. Now that you're my business partner, I want you to succeed in all your endeavors. When you're successful, so am I."

It was a logical explanation, but I didn't like it. "And that's the only reason you want to help me?" The TV was on in the background, but I tuned it out. A helicopter flew above the skyscrapers in the distance, but I didn't pay attention to it. I focused on the sound of her voice, her gentle breathing into the receiver.

"No..."

I'd never needed anyone's help. I didn't need her help. I always did everything alone, relying on my own instinct and experience. But the idea of bouncing ideas off of Titan, a woman far more intelligent than I was, sounded like a pleasure. "I'll be there in ten minutes."

OLD FASHIONS WERE IN FRONT OF US, AND WE HAD OUR work area set up at her kitchen table. Her overhead lights were dimmed low, the lights from the city bright enough to flood most of her penthouse. The smell of a meal wafted from the kitchen like she'd made something not too long ago.

I liked her cooking. It was better than the stuff my maid made for me.

Titan didn't make any sexy demands, getting right to work and switching into executive mode. "These guys are smart. All dropped out of Yale their sophomore year and built their company out of a storage bin."

"That sounds shitty."

"We were all there once." Her eyes scanned the computer screen, reading something. "Did you already schedule a meeting with them?"

"Right after lunchtime."

"Perfect. They'll be full and ready to listen."

I wrote down my offer number and slid it toward her. "What do you think of this?"

She stared at the figure as she pursed her lips together, that brilliant brain of hers working hard. "If it were me, I wouldn't be enticed by this. If they're meeting with you before your father, you have to make a strong impression. Be likable. Even flatter them."

I never flattered anyone with my offers. They could take it or leave it. Everyone knew I could turn their company into a corporation that would last a hundred years. "Just being in my presence is flattering enough."

The corner of her lip tugged into a smile. "Ordinarily, I would say you're right. But your father can offer the exact same thing you can offer. The only thing that can set you apart is compatibility."

"He's an asshole. We don't need to worry about that."

The corner of her lip fell. "Does he know you're a competitor?"

"No idea. But if he doesn't, he'll know tomorrow."

"Have you spoken to him?"

I never mentioned my father to Titan. She must have known about our bad blood from the web or gossip. "Not once in five years."

She nodded like she understood, even though she

couldn't have any comprehension of it. "Are you doing okay?"

"Why wouldn't I be okay?" I leaned back into the chair and stared her down hard, treating her like an enemy rather than my friend. Whenever this subject was broached, I was immediately defensive. It was in my blood now, this surge of hatred.

Titan slowly turned her head back to her screen. "I apologize for asking." Like nothing happened, she continued on with her work.

Now I was an asshole too. I was pumped full of so much hatred for that man, it turned me into a bitter and hateful person. Whenever he was on my mind, I couldn't think straight. The emotions were so complicated that I still hadn't sorted them out all these years later. Brett and I never spoke about him, a silent acknowledgment of mutual dislike. But Titan had opened up to me about a lot of things, like her father and her insomnia, in addition to intimate things that weren't confessed with words. She told me her mother abandoned her when I'd thought she was dead. She told me about her arrangement with Thorn. She still hadn't told me about her ex who died, but perhaps that would come in time. "I'm sorry, Titan. When it comes to my father...I turn into a different person."

She turned her face back to me, her features bathed

in the glow from the computer screen. When I dismissed her, she didn't seem cold. She took it with calm understanding. "We all have things we don't want to talk about. You don't need to apologize for it. I didn't mean to pry."

"You weren't prying."

She drank from her glass, letting the ice cubes hit her mouth and rest there. The ice rattled as she set the glass down on the table, the condensation immediately bubbling into the wood. She was in black leggings and a gray tee, comfortable around her home but not quite ready for bed even though it was almost midnight. "Do you really want this company? Or do you just not want your father to have it?"

I stared at her.

"I'm not judging. If this were an enemy of mine, I'd do the same thing. I'd do whatever I could to remind them who they were fucking with—and that they'd lose every time."

My defenses immediately came down. "It's a great business opportunity. If anyone else wanted the company, I'd still pursue it as aggressively. But now that he's the man I'm competing against, I have to win."

Titan nodded like she understood.

"He's not a good man... I know he's my father, but

that doesn't change anything." I drank from my glass, depleting it before returning it to the table.

"Just because someone is a parent doesn't make them a good person."

People often interjected their opinions about our relationship, saying it was unforgivable that a father turned on his son and vice versa. But people didn't know the true story, didn't understand how jealous and insecure my father was.

"May I ask what happened?"

No one else had ever asked me that question. They knew the topic was untouchable. "You can ask me anything, Titan." I didn't just feel that way because I wanted to know more about her. She'd earned my trust a long time ago. Something about her made me feel comfortable, made me feel like I could say anything. I didn't have to be the ruthless entrepreneur who wanted to crush everyone. With her, I could just be a man—blood, flesh, and muscle. "My mother had Brett before she met my father. My dad never liked Brett. Always treated him like trash. Jax and I always got the best gifts, the best education, everything. When my mother passed away, she didn't have any other relatives for Brett to go to...so he stayed with us. But my father was even more cruel to him. No presents on Christmas, put in the worst public school system in Brooklyn, sometimes no dinner... It never stopped. He hated Brett because my mother had loved someone before him. Took out all his jealousy on him...a fifteen-year-old. Time went on, and we got older. Brett moved out of the house and started living in a dump because he didn't have anything else. My father gave me my start in his company...but I couldn't take it anymore. I started helping Brett, letting him live with me, giving him a job. My father didn't like that. Told me and Jax we weren't allowed to have any more contact with him. He was an adult—and not part of our family. So my father made me choose. I could stay with him and work for a billion-dollar company that I would inherit with Jax someday...or I could choose Brett and lose everything. I chose Brett."

Titan's hard expression softened in the light of the computer screen. Her lips fell into a soft frown, and her eyes crinkled in the corners as the emotion seeped into her heart. Her hand slowly slid across the table until she found mine. Her soft skin brushed against mine in a gentle caress. Her thumb moved over my knuckles.

I stared at her hand, feeling how warm it was. Her skin was silky to the touch, and I could feel her gentle pulse. Her nails were elegantly painted with French tips. Her hands looked unblemished, even though she typed and wrote all day.

This touch wasn't as erotic as the ones I was used to.

Sometimes her nails dug into my shoulders, and she nearly cut into the skin. Sometimes her legs were wrapped tightly around my waist, keeping me in place and refusing to let me slide away. Sometimes her arms were wrapped around my neck as she kissed me—hard.

But this was my favorite touch of all.

It wasn't the touch of friendship or the touch of love.

Something better.

Something only we understood.

I turned my hand over so our palms were facing one another. My fingers interlocked with hers, and I gave her hand a squeeze. A lot of women had come and go in my life, but they were just women. Beautiful distractions. I'd never had a woman who was a friend—as close to me as Pine and Mike.

Now she was part of my inner circle.

"Whenever I talk about the things that happened to me, people always say they're sorry. But it never helps. It's a strange thing to say." She stared at our joined hands. "I want to say something like that to you now... but I can't find the words."

"It's okay," I whispered. "The thought is more powerful than anything you could say anyway."

She brought my hand to her face and kissed my fingers. She took her time, pressing each one against her soft lips. Then she cradled it against her cheek, turning affectionate. It was endearing, but more than anything else, it was sexy. She wasn't trying to be attractive. That was the last thing on her mind. But she made it happen anyway.

I should get back to work, but now I didn't care about tomorrow. Megaland and Vincent Hunt were the last things on my mind right now. All I could think about were those plump red lips, those soft fingertips, and that beautiful expression in her eyes.

All I could think about was Tatum.

I MET WITH THE THREE FOUNDERS OF MEGALAND. THEY were all exactly as Brett described them.

Brilliant minds with nerdy personalities.

When I asked what other plans they had in the works, they were mostly transparent in the new technology they were debuting. But they kept a few things under wraps because they didn't have a patent on it just yet.

The conversation went well, and then I laid my offer on the table—taking Titan's advice.

I started high, much higher than I ordinarily would.

When the guys looked at the offer, they did their best to cover up their surprise, but they didn't do a good enough job. A slight dilation in their eyes told me everything I wanted to know.

"In addition to this, I offer an unlimited amount of investment into your company. I don't intend to kick back and gain your profits. The opposite, actually. I want to elevate this company into an echelon that most tech companies only dream of. Not only do I have the money, but I also have the connections. I've been doing business for a long time. I think we would be great partners."

Nick, the main guy, stared at the paper again before he looked at his two friends.

They would be stupid not to take it.

They whispered in each other's ears then made some notes on the paper where I couldn't see.

I waited patiently on the other side of the table, sitting in their white conference room with black furniture. It was open and full of space, minimalistic. It was nothing like my own office, where I indulged in luxuries and dark tones. "What do you think, gentlemen? Do we have a deal?"

Nick was the one spoke for all the three of them. "We think it's a very generous offer. A lot more than we thought was going to be put on the table. We know you by reputation and think you'd be a great partner."

Too many words. "Is that a yes, then?"

"Not quite," Nick said. "We have a meeting with another investor later today."

Vincent Hunt. I had to handle this carefully. If my dad put his offer on the table, things would get ugly. If I could seal this deal before he had a chance to step into the office, it would be a slam dunk. My father probably didn't even know I was sitting in their office right this moment. I'd never shown interest in the tech sphere, so I probably didn't cross his mind. "I doubt your other investor will walk in with an offer like this."

"We don't know," Nick said. "But it's always best not to assume."

Clever. "I'm a very busy man. I'm sure you figured that out when you Googled me. I'm sure you also figured out that I'm not a man to fuck with."

It was so quiet I could hear a pin drop.

"I acquired Bruce Carol's company, and I've only had it for two weeks and its stock value has risen dramatically. When that asshole crossed me, all I had to do was tweet a message, and nobody would touch his company. I have something other investors will never have. Power. I have a lot of it, gentlemen."

They all listened, their shoulders slackening as they visibly leaned away.

"I'm the partner you want to have." I grabbed the paper I set on the table and pulled my pen from my pocket. I clicked the button before I scribbled a new offer onto the table. "I've nearly doubled my offer." I pushed the paper back toward them.

They looked like beetles with huge, bulging eyes.

"If you choose me as your partner right now, this is how much you get." I clicked the pen again and placed it back into my jacket pocket. "If you don't, my offer defaults to the original one I made. So, gentlemen, you're about to gamble. Play it safe and take this very generous offer now, or roll the dice. Maybe your other investor gives you more. Maybe he doesn't. There's a lot of money on the table. Choose wisely." I rose from the table and buttoned the front of my suit. "I'll give you one minute to talk it over." I walked out of the conference room without looking back and shut the door behind me. Then I stared at my watch, watching the second hand speed by.

Fifteen seconds.

Thirty seconds.

Forty-five seconds.

If they didn't take my offer, I'd be in deep shit. My father was ruthless. He would take it as a matter of pride to beat me out of the company. It would be a bloody war —with lots of casualties.

Sixty seconds.

I walked back into the conference room just as they hushed their voices and turned quiet.

I unbuttoned the front of my suit and sat down. "Hope you used your minute well."

Nick glanced at the other two before he extended his hand. "We'd love to work with you, Mr. Hunt."

Relief flooded through me, but I didn't let the look show on my face. I gave them my best executive smile, the kind I showed to the cameras outside restaurants and parties. I shook his hand firmly, excited for the backhand I'd just given my father. He'd be pissed, but deep down inside, he'd also have to respect me.

And accept his defeat.

"Excellent," I said. "Now it's time to make you rich."

"We're already rich," Nick said.

I didn't hold back the chuckle from escaping my lips. "Being a millionaire is not rich, boys. Being a billionaire is."

9

TITAN

I was at home when Hunt called.

"Hunt." I never greeted him with much more affection than that over the phone, having no idea who he was around at the time. Someone could overhear me if they were standing close enough, not that Hunt would purposely put himself in that position.

"Titan."

"How'd it go?" I'd been thinking about it all day, wondering if Hunt or his father got the deal. I didn't know Vincent Hunt, only his name and reputation, but I did know Diesel Hunt—and I believed in him. He had gifts that most men couldn't even begin to dream of.

And not just in the bedroom.

His smile was audible over the phone before he even said anything. "I got it."

I didn't care about the deals my peers made. I kept

track, but their successes and failures didn't mean anything to me. The only person I was invested in was myself. But hearing his accomplishment truly made me happy. "I'm not surprised. I knew you would make it happen." In that moment, as with several times prior, I knew Hunt was more than just some guy I was screwing. His well-being and happiness were essential for my own.

He was part of my inner circle.

"Thanks," he said. "I gave them the large offer up front, and they bit."

"And?"

"I told them I'd give them an even bigger offer if they took my offer then and there. If they met with anyone else, they would get my smaller offer."

I was impressed, and that was something that didn't happen often. "Genius."

"And they took it. I gave them a gambling metaphor. Smart guys don't gamble. It's not in their nature. It did the trick."

"Awesome."

"I paid more than I wanted...but I'm sure my father is ticked."

"He should be," I said. "Not only did he lose a viable business opportunity, but he was outsmarted by a man

half his age. Arrogant men always get what's coming
to them..."

"We both know I'm arrogant."

"Maybe that was a not so subtle hint..."

He chuckled. "I'm coming over."

I didn't invite him, but I didn't object. If he didn't
volunteer his presence, I would have just asked for it
anyway. "I'll make dinner."

"Are we celebrating?" he asked. "I love your
cooking."

"You do?" I knew a few things around the kitchen,
but I definitely didn't have the skills to impress anyone.

"Definitely. Better than my maid's."

"Then you need to get a new maid," I said with a laugh.

"Don't underestimate yourself. You succeed at
anything you put your mind to."

"But I've never been motivated in the culinary arts."

I heard him speak to his driver before he got into the
back seat. "Then why don't you hire someone to prepare
your meals for you?"

"I don't want anyone in my penthouse."

Hunt paused for a few seconds, the quiet sound of
the radio on in the background. "So you clean your
entire place?"

"Yep."

"That's how paranoid you are?"

I didn't appreciate that word. "I'm not paranoid. I just value my privacy."

"What about your other places?"

"Yes, those are taken care of around the clock. But my penthouse is different."

Hunt stayed on the phone with me until the car pulled up in front of my building. Even when he didn't have anything to say, he stayed on the line. "What are you hiding?"

"Who says I'm hiding anything?"

He chuckled. "The richest woman in the world doesn't clean her own place because she's that down-to-earth..."

Yes, I did have secrets. "Okay...maybe I do have a few secrets. A few skeletons in my closet."

"You let me come over."

"Because you're the skeleton."

The door shut behind him, and he walked into the building. The elevator dinged when he entered the passcode and rode up to the top floor. Hunt was quiet for a while before he said something else. "What other skeletons do you have?"

The elevator doors opened and revealed him standing in the center. I looked directly at him, seeing his mocha-colored eyes staring back at me.

He stepped inside with the phone still pressed to his ear.

I continued to hold mine. "You don't want to know." I hung up and set the phone on the table.

Hunt slid his into his pocket. He was in a suit, obviously skipping the gym and coming here instead. He walked up to me and cupped my face before he kissed me on the mouth. His soft lips brushed against mine before his tongue moved into my mouth. His fingers yanked on my hair slightly as he moved farther into me. The kiss seemed to last only ten seconds even though it was minutes. Then he pulled away. "I do want to know."

I didn't understand his statement at all because all I'd been thinking about was that kiss. After a few seconds of thinking, I remembered the last thing we were talking about. "The less you know, the better." My hand ran down his chest before I walked into the kitchen. "How's sweet butternut stew?"

He followed behind me and joined me at the counter. "No idea what that is."

"It's a vegan stew I make. It's pretty good. It's got sweet potatoes and butternut squash, mixed with red lentils and white rice."

"Actually, that doesn't sound bad."

"You want to help me?"

Any other guy would rather park his ass on the

couch and turn on football, but he smiled in response. "I'd love to."

"Do you know how to peel potatoes?"

"I can make you come three times in a row," he said sarcastically. "Yes, I can peel a potato."

"Sex is much easier when you look like that." I patted his ass on the way to the fridge.

He gave me that rugged smile that was mixed with boyish charm. "You like my ass, baby?"

He called me baby again. And again, I said nothing. "I wanted to dig my teeth into it the first time I saw it."

"There's still time." He smacked his own ass playfully.

"Be careful what you wish for."

We diced the vegetables and prepared them in the hot pans. We added ingredients, prepared the rice, and sautéed vegetables to go with it. Working in comfortable unison, it was like we'd done this several times.

"Do you think your dad knows by now?"

"Oh yeah," he said. "The guys at Megaland must have given him the courtesy of canceling."

"But they may not have given up your identity."

"They wouldn't have to. He'll figure it out."

We combined the rice and the stew together into big bowls, making more than enough for both of us. We carried them to the kitchen table along with two Old

Fashioneds. We sat down and ate, picking up the conversation.

"Have you been in the same room together since you last spoke?" I asked.

"A few times. He doesn't look at me. I don't look at him."

I understood Hunt's decision, but I thought the situation was terribly sad at the same time. Hunt still had his father around, but the man was pretty much dead to him. I didn't have any either of my parents anymore. I'd made a great life for myself and I didn't need anyone, but any son or daughter would always need their parents—or at least want them. "He's never contacted you?"

"No."

"Have you ever considered calling him?"

He kept eating, taking his time as he chewed his bites. "No."

"What about your brother?"

"Jax and I don't talk either. We don't have any beef. We're just on different sides of the same war."

"That's too bad."

"But I don't respect him," Hunt said. "Brett is our brother, even if only half his blood is the same as ours. Jax turned the other cheek while my father treated him like garbage. That's not okay to me."

I always respected those who rooted for the under-dog. If people hadn't done the same to me, I wouldn't be here now. A lot of people tried to undercut me, but a lot of people lifted me up too. "I know it's not my place to say anything, but I think that's really sweet. Your mom would be proud of you."

He flinched slightly at the mention of his mother. His hand halted as he gripped the spoon. Then he scooped up another bite like nothing had happened. "I don't know what my mother would think of me. But I know she would be disappointed in my father for dividing us like this."

"I know she wouldn't be disappointed in you. If you weren't divided, then Brett would be an outcast. That's the last thing she would have wanted."

"Maybe." He kept eating without looking at me, his exterior cold.

I assumed he didn't want to talk about his mom anymore, but there was one more thing I wanted to say. "Brett told me about her accident. I know it was a long time ago, and this doesn't help at all, but I'm sorry."

He turned his gaze slowly back on to me, his brown eyes darker than they were before. He seemed angry and touched at the same time. "Thanks...I'm surprised he told you that."

I didn't reveal the rest he told me. "I can't remember how it came up."

He finished his food, wiping the bowl clean. "That was great. Thank you."

"And thank you. You helped me."

"Team effort." He pushed his bowl aside and took a drink of his Old Fashioned. He stirred the ice cubes before he took another sip. "We've been talking about me all night. What about you?"

"What about me?" I crossed my legs and plucked the cherry out of my drink. I popped it into my mouth and yanked the stem out, dropping it onto the napkin.

"How was your day?"

"The same as all the others."

"You seem bored."

"Quite the opposite. I have to fly to California for a meeting next week. Not looking forward to that."

"Why? You have a place there, right?"

"I just have so much to do here."

She might have to reschedule that meeting. I wasn't giving up a single day during my six weeks.

"And then Thorn wants to take a trip to visit his parents in Chicago."

She just saw them. That was something else that would have to change during our six weeks.

"My assistant is getting better. She was terrible in the beginning, but now she owns it."

"It was nice of you to be patient with her."

"People were patient with me, once upon a time."

"I can't picture a version of you that's anything other than perfect at everything."

Both corners of her mouth rose in a smile. "Oh, she definitely exists."

He glanced at my private wet bar before he turned back to me. "How many does it take to knock you over?"

"Nothing knocks me over."

"You've never been drunk?" he asked incredulously.

"No. I don't like losing control of my faculties. A buzz is nice, but nothing more than that."

"And how many do you drink a day to get there?"

"Hmm…" I stirred my glass as I thought about his question. "Ten."

He couldn't hide his skeptical look. "You can drink ten of these a day?"

"I could, but I don't."

"How many do you usually have?"

I shrugged as I thought about it. "Probably five."

He still seemed surprised by that. "I drink a lot, but you do laps around me."

"I hardly believe that."

"Well, I don't drink during the week. I can only take in so many calories."

"I can because I just don't eat."

"Yeah, I've noticed," he said darkly.

I was done with the chitchat, our stomachs full and our conversation over. "You still want to see one of my secrets?" I pushed my empty glass away and stood up, my fingertips still resting on the surface of the table.

His face shifted up to look at me, his eyes greedy for knowledge. "Yes."

My hand went to his shoulder, and I gave it a tight squeeze. "Then follow me." I led the way, leaving the living room and moving into the hallway. My feet clapped against the hardwood floor, and I could hear his heavy footsteps behind me. I turned right down a different hallway, leading him to a side of my penthouse he'd never seen before.

The door was white like all the others. To anybody passing by, it would seem uninteresting, a door that led to another bathroom or closet. But it led to somewhere truly spectacular.

I walked inside first, stepping into the dark room with chains, whips, and ropes. I flicked on the lights, revealing the display cases with tools I mostly collected, never used. Unlike other playrooms I'd seen, mine was in tones of white and gray, matching the rest of my fortress. It was feminine but powerful.

Hunt stepped inside and swept across the room with his eyes. He examined the chains in the ceiling, the gray mat in the center of the floor, and the case full of whips in various sizes. His hands sat in the pockets of his slacks. His jaw was harder than usual, and his eyes weren't burning with anger like they sometimes did.

Indifference.

He wasn't the least bit intimidated.

Not even slightly annoyed.

He brushed his fingers along one of the whips before he walked onto the soft pad on the floor. His eyes found mine as he moved his hands to his neck and yanked his tie off. Then he unbuttoned his shirt, letting it fall open little by little.

It took a lot to get my heart beating in this room. I'd seen it all. I'd done everything. But watching Hunt undress himself, not recoiling in disgust, was the sexiest thing I'd ever seen. He not only accepted my challenge —but he raised it with his own.

I licked my lips.

My throat went dry.

My entire body ached for this man.

This fearless man.

He moved to his pants next and kicked off his shoes.

He stripped down to his black boxers, muscular thighs leading to toned legs. His thin waist had a sharp V from the indents of muscles. He looked just like a muscle car, full of masculine curves and a powerful engine.

His back was tight against his waist and extended to a powerful pair of shoulders. Muscles etched in stone were across his skin, an endless array of power all along his back. His triceps were cut, his biceps jutting out in the opposite direction.

The look he wore was sexier than the rest of him. His jaw had a slight shadow, but it was enough to darken his features. His brown eyes contrasted against his fair skin, his brown hair still perfectly styled because I hadn't dug my fingers into it yet.

I was the one who owned this room, but he quickly hijacked it. "I'm ready, Boss Lady."

My spine tightened then shivered.

He was obedient, but only in his own way. He gave me the floor, but he determined the timetable. I was the one in charge, but he was still pulling the strings. It was discreet, subtle enough that I may not have noticed.

But I did notice.

"I'm not. On your knees." I stood in front of him, my arms resting by my sides.

Hunt stared at me without blinking, his muscular arms tight as they hung by his hips.

I kept my harsh gaze, commanding him without speaking.

He still didn't move.

"Don't make me ask you again."

"Four days."

I heard what he said and knew exactly what it meant. In four days, all of this would be over. I would be the one who was ordered around. I might as well enjoy this moment as much as I could—because it was about to be a memory.

Before I could ask him again, he lowered himself to his knees.

And I experienced a high like I'd never known before. I'd never been with a man who challenged me so much, who earned my respect so quickly. I'd never been with a man and cared about his life outside my bed. Now Hunt and I had lives that were intricately intertwined. "Stay." I walked out of the playroom and raided my closet. I found the teddy and garters I wanted to wear, along with the sky-high black heels that made my ass look plump. I walked back into the playroom a moment later.

Hunt was still on his knees, and his eyes roamed over me greedily. His jaw started to tighten, the same reaction he gave when he was either angry or lustful. Right now, I knew which emotion it was.

I walked to the display case and grabbed one of my crops, one of the soft and slender ones. I felt the leather against my palm before I turned back to him.

Hunt stared at the implement. "Are you going to hit me with that?"

I smacked the end against my own palm, making a quiet snapping noise. "Yes."

"You're going to have to use something bigger than that."

I couldn't control the shock on my face. Hunt continued to surprise me, to catch me off-balance without even trying. I returned the crop and grabbed a flogger instead.

Hunt shook his head. "Grab a whip, baby."

I ran the tips of the flogger over my hand, humbled once again. I tossed the flogger on the floor and grabbed one of my bullwhips. It was long with an incredible snap. "This is going to hurt, Hunt."

"I hope it does."

I didn't see a hint of fear on his face.

"Do your worst, baby. In four days, I'll do mine."

If I lingered on that sentence too long, I would lose my nerve. I looked forward to doing whatever I wanted to him, but I feared the unknown. I feared being the one to obey, to be at the mercy of this man. No matter how bad it was, I couldn't walk away. He committed to everything I asked. It would be unfair for me to bow out.

I walked behind him and brushed the whip across his back, teasing him. He didn't flinch at the touch. His breathing didn't even increase. Everything stayed exactly the same. If he was anxious for the pain, he didn't show it. "It won't scar you."

"Doesn't matter if it does."

No matter what I said, he challenged me. He gave me the control, but in a very small form. I pulled my whip back, preparing to strike him. "I'm gonna hit you ten times, Hunt. And when I'm finished—"

"Make it twenty."

I was turned on by his eagerness but also dismayed. "Don't interrupt me."

Silence.

"When I'm done, we're going to have even more fun." I struck the whip across his back, immediately reddening the skin at the impact. "Count with me."

His deep voice was steady. His body didn't sway with the momentum of the hit. "One."

Hearing that masculine voice sent shivers all down my body. He asked for twenty lashes, but I wasn't sure I could wait that long. My thighs ached to wrap around his waist, to feel his thick cock pound me until he hit my trigger. I whipped again, a little harder.

"Two."

I'd never been whipped, but I knew it hurt. His lack of response was impressive. I usually got a moan or a cringe from my other lovers. I'd never been greeted with silence. I struck him a few more times, bringing our total up to ten.

We were halfway there, but he hadn't broken a sweat. He hadn't changed his position despite the strain on his knees. His arms remained directly at his sides, his hands open and not tight in a fist.

I slashed the whip across his back.

"Eleven." His voice was exactly the same as it was before. I suspected it would be the same until we finished.

Every single slash was greeted with the same reaction. Like the bite of the leather had no effect on him at all, he held his body perfectly straight and didn't lean forward with the heat. His breathing never escalated. If anything, it slowed down. His back was marked with red lines, marks that would fade in a few days.

I continued on, finally getting to twenty.

And he didn't move.

I threw the whip down, hot and covered in sweat from striking him. My body ached for his in the most powerful way I'd ever known. This man was immune to pain, untouched by any stimuli that he didn't want to be affected by. He had complete control over his mind, over his body. "Up."

He rose to his feet, not turning around.

I grabbed a chair from the wall and pulled it to the center of the room. "Sit."

He took a seat, his expression stoic.

With a single rope, I secured his legs to the chair and tied his arms together in the back. When he couldn't move at all, even thrust his hips upward, I yanked down his boxers, unfastened my crotch, and straddled his hips.

I lowered myself onto his length, my warm cream sheathing him all the way to the base.

He immediately tugged on the ropes as he released an angry growl. His eyebrow ridges came together, and he grinded his teeth. His dark eyes matched the color of the chair, deep with a violent flare.

I sank all the way down, taking in his length until I could feel him stretch my walls apart. His skin was reddened from the aggressive thickness of the leather, and I liked seeing his body marked up. I dragged my tongue across his shoulder then kissed his neck.

His hands yanked on the ropes again.

I gripped the back of the chair and positioned myself on my feet. His cock was long enough that I could pull it off, rise up and sheathe his dick again. The first time I met him, I suspected he was packing.

And he definitely was.

"Jesus, I already want to come..." He leaned his face forward and kissed my tits, his tongue catching the hard tip and running through the valley between my breasts. Sometimes he sucked the skin into his mouth, brushing it against the hardness of his teeth. He breathed across my skin, the excitement in his voice loud.

"Better not." I bounced up and down, gripping his shoulders for balance.

He looked past me and stared into the mirror on the opposite wall, having a great view of my ass as it moved up and down. He watched me move, his breathing deep and shaky. His shoulders shifted forward as he tried to break through the tight ropes.

"You aren't going anywhere." I sat on his dick and gave him a slow kiss. "Not until I'm finished."

He breathed into my mouth. "I never want to go anywhere, Boss Lady."

I kissed his jawline, feeling the thick hair brush against my soft lips. My hand dug into his hair as I kept moving, sliding down his cock over and over. I was the one on top, the one calling the shots, but it somehow felt equal, felt like we were in this together. I only conquered him because he allowed me to, wanted me to, was man enough to let it happen.

And I was about to do the same to him.

I already felt the orgasm starting, building in my gut as the sensations spread out everywhere. My nerves were on fire, my mouth parched. I felt my body tightening in preparation of what was about to happen. Hunt always made me come good and hard, even when I was the one doing all the work. He let me use his glorious body to fulfill my needs. He gave me exactly what I needed. "Yes..."

He stared into my eyes and watched the performance unfold. "Come all over my dick, baby..."

I rode his length harder, quickening my pace and losing my breath in the process. I closed my eyes and let out a scream that could rupture Hunt's eardrums. Moisture sheathed his length all the way down to his balls and dripped onto the chair.

"When's it gonna be my turn, Boss Lady?" he whispered against my mouth.

"Not anytime soon." I was gonna ride this cock until I couldn't handle it anymore. I wasn't getting off him until my pussy was stretched and sore. I only had a few days left with him, when I had all the power. It would be a painful goodbye, a crippling transition of power. I wouldn't be able to tie him up anymore, to whip him until his beautiful skin was marked. I'd be at his mercy.

So I was going to keep him at my mercy for a little bit longer.

WE STOOD IN THE SHOWER TOGETHER, THE WARM WATER rinsing away the soap. I washed my hair even though it was in great shape after our rough rendezvous. I just loved being under the warm water, letting it comfort me in a column of white noise. Since I was just going to shower again in the morning, I didn't see the harm. My mascara and foundation were washed away. My lipstick disappeared a long time ago, somewhere on Hunt's mouth.

Hunt moved underneath the water, discreetly pushing me out of the stream of water with his size. The shower washed away his shampoo, and he turned his back to me. Lines of red marks were on either side of his flank. His flesh was irritated in the areas that covered the most muscle, the blood rushing to the surface to heal the injury. The sight turned me on, but it also made me feel guilty for what I'd done. "I have some cream you can put on that."

"Don't need any."

"The marks will heal faster."

He dragged his hands down his face. "I'm not in a hurry."

He refused to show pain or discomfort in front of me, either because he was trying to prove a point or because he was truly resilient to the pain.

I respected him for it, and I knew he would expect the same from me once the tables were turned. "Not everyone reacts so calmly when they see that room. Some ask what's wrong with me...others just walk out."

He ran his hands through his dark hair, his eyes on me.

"But you didn't seem to think anything."

"I've heard of the BDSM lifestyle."

"Not just because of that...but because I'm a woman."

"You know exactly what you want, what you're into. Why would I judge you for that?"

Was he the greatest man on the planet? God's gift to all women?

"I obviously wouldn't have participated in that unless I was getting something out of it."

"So you didn't enjoy it?" I asked quietly, trying to hide my disappointment.

"No, I did. Surprisingly. But I would have enjoyed it more if I were the one holding the whip."

I was standing in the humid shower, but I suddenly felt ice-cold. An earthquake erupted inside me, my panic breaking through the crust of my skin. I felt the earth shake even though I was perfectly still.

I didn't think. I just moved.

I walked out of the shower and pulled the towel around my body. My bare feet made wet footsteps all the way across the tile and into the bedroom. I pulled the towel over my shoulders, and I walked to the window where I had a clear view of the city.

I stared at the lights and blocked out all my thoughts. I meditated, seeing the slight reflection of my face in the glass. The lights twinkled just like stars in the sky. There were millions of people in this city, living their lives. I thought about the trains on the subway, the cars sitting in traffic, of people still getting coffee from Starbucks at ten in the evening.

I thought about nothing of significance.

Footsteps sounded behind me. They grew in volume as he approached me, walking across my bedroom to where I stood in front of the window. He came up behind me and pressed his forehead against the back of my neck.

I'd brought myself to a state of calm, but now I was charged all over again. My blood was pumping, all the veins in my body swollen. I was aroused anytime he was near, but now I felt something else entirely.

A feeling I never showed.

"Tatum." His hands gripped both of my arms, just below the shoulder. He pressed his bare chest against my back, his heat hidden because of the towel wrapped around me. I could see him standing in just his slacks in the reflection, his hips narrow and his torso expanding into the powerful V.

I looked at his eyes in the reflection in the glass.

"Tell me."

"There's nothing to tell..." I'd let the fear get to me, but once I calmed myself down, I had returned to a state of serenity. I didn't show anger, fear, or spite in front of witnesses. With someone as famous as me, one who represented womankind everywhere, the slightest hint of weakness was judged more harshly than the same sin committed by a man.

"I saw the way you turned pale. And now I see you... soaking wet in front of a window." He squeezed my arms before he gently turned me in a circle, forcing me to face him. Now the city was in the background, and I was face-to-face with the man with the most captivating eyes. He was a warm morning on a fall day, his eyes espresso beans. Barefoot and bare-chested, he was nothing but solid man.

Looking at him made me forget what we were discussing. Made me forget what terrified me.

His hand grazed up my arm, over my shoulder, and up my neck. His large hand cupped my face, his thumb brushing across my bottom lip. It rested in the corner, his other fingers giving my neck a gentle squeeze. "Tell me what you're afraid of."

"I'm not afraid of anything." It was practically my mantra, to represent strength and never weakness. Of all people in this world, I should be able to take down my walls for him. But even then, I still couldn't do it. Only one person truly understood my fears, had witnessed them himself.

"We're all afraid of something. You're no different."

"That's where you're wrong..."

He tilted his head slightly, getting a better look at me. "I'm afraid to let anyone get too close. I'm afraid if I do, it'll just be another person that I'll lose. I've lost my mother when she was too young to die. I lost my father when he turned his back on me. And I lost my younger brother when he chose to side with a ruthless man. I'm bored by the women who sleep in my bed, but I'm too scared to have anything real. If I ever fell in love and I lost her...that would be the final straw." His thumb brushed across my cheek as he gazed deep into my eyes.

He put his true self on a platter, opened himself up to me.

Now it was my turn.

But I couldn't tell him. I couldn't confess my secret, a secret I'd been hiding for nearly a decade. I did my best to bury it in the past, to let the winds of time cover it with dust. To stick a shovel into the soil and unearth it... was like opening Pandora's box.

Hunt didn't show his frustration. "If you tell me, I'll understand you better. And if I understand you, I'll know exactly what to give you."

My eyes shifted to the floor, unable to meet his gaze. I refused to answer him, refused to part with the knowledge of that terrible time. I just wanted to move on and forget about it, to let it die in the past. If I didn't, it would haunt me constantly. I had to get over it—and I had to do it now. "Thank you for your sentiment, but I'm fine." I moved away from his embrace and patted my hair dry with the towel. I didn't look at him as I tried to brush off the conversation and return the atmosphere to casual. "I should probably get to bed soon. I have a lot of work to do in the morning."

"So, we're gonna pretend that you didn't just storm out of the shower?" Hunt walked up behind me again, his presence looming over me. There wasn't a shadow in the bedroom at this time of night, but I could certainly feel one.

"Nothing happened, Hunt. I walked away."

"You had a panic attack. I know you a lot better than you give me credit for."

"That was not a panic attack." I dropped the towel on the floor and grabbed a t-shirt and panties from my drawer. "If you classify it as that, you should see what I look like when I'm actually upset."

"They're one and the same."

I pulled the t-shirt over my head and the panties up my legs before I turned around. "Hunt, I think you should leave."

He smiled when there was nothing charming about this conversation. "And I think I just hit a pressure point."

My entire body tightened at his aggression. "Excuse me?"

"I've known for you three months now, Titan. I've been fucking you for six weeks. I was under the impression we were friends. I was under the impression you trusted me."

"Yes, but—"

"I was also under the impression that there was nothing but honesty between us. You obviously have some kind of trigger, but you refuse to share it with me —your partner. That's dishonest."

"It's not a trigger…"

"Then what the hell is it?" he snapped. "What makes you run away every time I mention being in control?"

"I told you I just have control issues. It's nothing I can't handle."

His eyes shifted back and forth as he looked into mine. "Why do you have to handle it at all, Titan?"

My lips pressed tightly together.

"Talk to me. I've told you everything about myself… but I still don't know anything about you."

"That's not true."

"Then prove it," he said. "Tell me about your late boyfriend."

I did a double take when I heard him hit the nail right on the head. He knew about my secret, just not the details. And face-to-face, he was asking me about it. He'd put me on the spot, making me feel more exposed than I could remember. I made sure that information was wiped from the news. I made sure all the details were covered up and hidden away. I made sure the judge sealed the documents. The only way anyone could access them was if they pulled some strings.

And Hunt could pull strings.

"I may have Googled you once or twice to know

more about you, your business relationships and your ambitions. But never did I stick my nose into your private life. I never asked your brother about your mother. He told me that on his own. You have no right—"

"I've never done that, Titan. I've never dug around in your closet and searched for your skeletons. The only reason why I know about your boyfriend is because Pine's father knew you at the time. Pine brought it up to me a few months ago. That's all I know. I swear on my mother's grave."

Now that I knew my business was my own, my claws retracted back into my fingertips. I sheathed my anger like a giant sword. I controlled my temper, reminding myself that I genuinely adored the man standing right in front of me.

"I could access all of that information if I wanted to." His voice turned quiet, his rage finally simmering as mine was. "But I don't want a report on my desk. I want to hear it from you. And until you tell me...I'll never know."

Most people didn't know about Jeremy because it was long before I'd made a name for myself. It wasn't even listed on my Wikipedia page. It was something I hid inside a dark basement because it would change the world's perception of me—for many reasons. The fact that he knew there was more there but refused to pry made my respect for him grow even more. "Thank you."

His arms circled my waist, and he pulled me close to his body. "Will you ever tell me?"

The second I told someone, I risked that information coming back to bite me in the ass. I risked putting it out for the general public to know. What if Hunt and I had a fight, and he wanted to betray me? What if our business arrangement went south, and he wanted to hurt me? None of those scenarios seemed likely. "Maybe…"

"Maybe is better than no. I'll take it." He pressed his lips to my forehead, giving me a soft kiss filled with heat. His powerful arms turned into a cage around my body, protecting me from the outside world.

When I was in his cage, I actually felt safe.

"Four more days," he whispered, like there was any possibility of me forgetting.

"Four days…"

I LET MYSELF INTO THORN'S PENTHOUSE. "IT'S ME." I TOLD him I was coming by, but I didn't want to walk in on him with a woman on the couch.

It had happened before.

"In the kitchen."

I set my purse down then joined him. "What are you making?"

"Tacos. You hungry?"

"I'm always hungry because I don't eat."

He smiled before he turned off the stove. "Excellent point. Are you not eating now?"

The grilled chicken, rice, and beans looked delicious. "No, this looks pretty damn good."

"Good. Because I can't eat all of this by myself. The ladies wouldn't like me if I did."

We made our tacos before we took them to the dining room.

He grabbed himself a beer before he quickly threw together an Old Fashioned for me. We sat together at the table and squeezed the lime all over our food. "So, only a few days left, right?"

Thorn must have figured out it was on my mind. "Two days."

"Are you ready?"

I took a long drink of my Old Fashioned, appreciating the whiskey as it traveled down my throat and into my belly. "As ready as I'll ever be…I suppose."

"I'm sure you'll be fine, Titan. Just don't overthink it. Enjoy it." Thorn's encouragement was somehow suspicious considering he was an eyewitness to everything I'd been through.

"What makes you think I'd enjoy it?"

"Because a lot of people do. You enjoy making him submit. And I bet he enjoyed having a woman over-power him like that. Imagine some hot man taking all of the control? Taking all the weight of decision-making off your shoulders? You would walk into that room and only be concerned with how much you were going to be pleased."

Now my suspicions were at an all-time high. "Hunt told me you encouraged him to keep pursuing me, even when things seemed bleak."

He shrugged. "You're my friend. I want you to get laid."

"But you also hate him."

"Never said that." He grabbed a taco with a single hand and ate nearly the entire thing.

"So what's the deal, Thorn? Why are you pushing this so hard?"

"I'm not pushing anything," he said. "I just think you need to move on."

"Move on?"

"Yes. It's been nearly ten years since that shit with Jeremy. Let's leave it in the past and forget about it. Being a sub isn't going to be anything like the way it was with him. It doesn't seem like your relationship even resembles that."

I mostly just teased Hunt, made him fuck me the way I liked. There weren't many chains or whips, not like there were with my other partners. I was satisfied having him in my bed, taking it nice and slow so I could appreciate every inch of that hard cock. "Not really."

"You're just overthinking it. Hunt is a good guy. He's not gonna hurt you."

"Maybe you do like him."

"I never said I disliked the guy. I just don't like the fact that he likes you so much. That's my only problem with him."

"Well, I asked him about it, and he denied your claims."

"Then I've got nothing to worry about." He picked up his other taco. "Worse come to worst, you can just walk away, Titan. He can't keep you there, even though he stayed the whole time. You always have a way out."

"But I don't want a way out..." I didn't want to walk away from Hunt, not when we had this special connection, not when I was getting incredible sex on a daily basis. If he left, I would miss him.

I couldn't deny that.

"Then tough it out," Thorn said. "I know you can do that."

I hadn't taken a bite of my food yet, so I scooped one taco into my hand. My eyes turned to the window, seeing the sky start to fade to black. "What's new with you?"

"Nothing really. Mom keeps pestering me about proposing to you."

"Wow, she really likes me."

"She adores you." He rolled his eyes. "You're all she ever talks about. When she called me the other day, the first question that came out of her mouth was literally about you. No hi... No, how are you? Right down to business."

I laughed before I took a bite. "That's flattering."

"And annoying."

"Are you jealous?" I asked.

"Psh, no." He kept eating. "But I told her it wasn't going to be for a while. That's when she started asking about grandkids and shit...gives me a headache."

"Our kids will be cute."

"Because they'll look like me?" he teased.

"No. Because they'll be loved so much. They've got you and me and two grandparents who will cherish them until it drives them crazy. They'll never know what it's like to be hungry or financially unsteady. They'll have so much...and they won't even know it." Money had always been an issue for my father and me when I was young. Thorn was born into a rich family, so he had no idea what being broke was even like.

He patted his hand on mine. "And they'll be cute... because they'll look like you."

Having children was one of my guilty pleasures. I had been deemed a hard-ass executive who only cared about money, but I had a calling to be a mother. I wanted a family of my own since there wasn't a single living Titan around. It was something I needed. "Thank you."

He patted my hand again before he pulled his away. "And I'll have a lot of fun making them with you."

"Thorn." I rolled my eyes, not surprised by the inappropriate comment.

"What?" he asked innocently. "You know the sex is gonna be fantastic."

I felt guilty talking about having sex with another man when I was committed to Hunt at the moment. Hunt knew it was going to happen. I'd revealed the truth to him a while ago, so it wasn't like it was a secret. But we were still jumping ahead. "Even so..."

"You know we're gonna have a blast being married. At least, I am."

10

HUNT

ONE MORE DAY.

One more day and my life would never be the same.

Titan would be mine.

Completely. Utterly. Eternally.

I'd have her when I wanted her. Fuck her exactly how I desired. And possess her in a way I never had before.

She was mine.

We hadn't made another trip to her playroom again. When I'd walked inside, it was exactly as I'd imagined it would be. I'd been inside a BDSM club before. I wasn't a participant in the lifestyle, but I'd been with women who were. They asked me to fuck them while they wore gas masks, a bar spreader between their legs... If a woman wanted to be fucked in a kinky way, no way in hell was I going to say no. However she wanted it, I would give it to her.

But I made a bigger exception for Titan.

I considered it to be an investment. I put in my time, accepted things I normally wouldn't, and now I was being rewarded.

By making Titan into my woman.

I eyed the clock on my computer screen as I sat in my office. I just had two meetings, skipped lunch, and I was supposed to play golf with a potential client later. But I'd have to reschedule that.

Because, at midnight, I had plans.

When the clock struck twelve, my six weeks would begin. There would be lots of sex, lots of obedience, and lots of the kinky shit I was into. I'd paid my dues, and now it was my turn to order her to her knees.

To seize the control.

My fingers rested against each other as I stared out the window of my office, my mind slipping into my perverted fantasies of Tatum Titan. I was harder than steel, but I'd had her enough times to feel satisfied and subdued. I shouldn't want her even more. I shouldn't have this much blood pumping in my veins, feel this kind of adrenaline.

Not for a woman I'd already had.

But I did. I craved her like a drug. Craved her like I would never get enough.

Natalie's voice came through the intercom. "Sir, I have Jax Hunt on the line." Her voice suggested she knew exactly who that was—and this was a strange phone call.

I stared at the speaker where her voice came from, but I didn't respond. I hadn't spoken to my younger brother in over five years. I crossed paths with him once at a bar, but we pretended not to see each other. We were two men who picked two different sides, but we didn't have any beef with one another.

It was sad.

"Sir?" Natalie caught my attention before my mind slipped away too far.

I straightened in my chair. "I'll take it."

"Sending the call through."

The phone rang. I would normally put it on speaker-phone because hands-free was always easier. I was only half paying attention to what someone said anyway, writing an email at the same time. But this time, all of my focus was on the conversation. I took the call and pressed the phone to my ear.

I hadn't said a word to my brother in years. There wasn't a single sentence I could say to reflect the chasm in our relationship. The man was practically a stranger.

The only reason why I knew he was still single with no kids was because it would have been all over the news if he settled down. I said the safest words that came to mind. "Jax. How can I help you?" I didn't know what I would be met with. Resentfulness. Rage. Indifference. No way to tell until he said something.

His voice was just as steady as mine. "Our father is pretty pissed about Megaland."

I didn't need his confirmation to know that.

"He's seeing red right now."

Redundant. "I wanted that company to the exclusion of all else. It didn't matter who my competitor was."

"He doesn't see it that way."

Jax stuck to business, which didn't surprise me. I stuck to business too.

"You shouldn't have crossed him, Diesel."

"It's just business, Jax. He knows that better than anyone."

"That's not how he's taking it."

I rested my elbows on the desk as I listened, the city silent around me even though it was thriving with constant life. "Why are you telling me this?"

"Because he sees it as a declaration of war. Thought you should know the battle has begun."

My fingers drummed on the desk. My father and I had a mutual dislike for each other, but we never went out of our way to spite one another. But this was obviously different to him. I knew it about his pride and nothing else. "I still don't know why you're telling me this, Jax. If you expect me to apologize, I won't. If you expect me to bow out and give him the company, I won't do that either."

"No, I wasn't expecting any of that," he said. "I'm just..." His voice trailed away, and we both sat on the phone in silence.

I listened to the pause, waiting for words. Hoping for words.

"I just wanted to warn you."

TEN MINUTES BEFORE MIDNIGHT, MY DRIVER DROVE ME across town until I arrived in front of her building. The fall chill was starting to creep into the air, making the windows fog. I wore a hoodie when I would normally just wear a t-shirt.

The car stopped, and I pulled my bag over my shoulder before I stepped out.

Just then, the front door to the lobby opened.

And Bruce Carol walked out. He was unmistakable with his bushy eyebrows and pouty lips. His eyebrows ridges looked like mountains. He wore a thick black jacket with the collar popped, either to hide his appearance or protect his neck from the cold.

What the fuck?

He walked to a black car parked at the curb on the other side of the street. The taillights were red, and steam was coming out of the exhaust pipe. Someone was in the driver's seat, and as soon as Bruce was in the rear, he drove off.

I wasn't sure what I saw.

Did he live in this building?

It was possible. The building was full of the rich elites of New York City. There were probably other people I knew who lived in the building. I just never crossed paths with them because I always went to the private elevator.

After relieving myself of my paranoia, I walked inside and got into the elevator. I didn't tell Titan I was coming. At the stroke of midnight, I wouldn't need permission or explanations. I could do whatever the hell I wanted—when I wanted.

I rode the elevator to the top, and the doors opened into her dark living room. Most of the lights were off, so she must already be in bed. I stepped inside and walked down the hallway. It was quiet, and the elevators doors closed with a ding.

She must know I was here.

I walked in through the open doorway of her bedroom and found her standing in front of the floor-to-ceiling windows. Her arms were crossed over her chest, and she stood in just a black thong. It was dark, so I could only distinguish her silhouette.

I took a moment to look at her, to enjoy the sight of her quiet reserve. I turned my wrist and watched the time.

One minute.

I set my bag down and walked farther into the room, the darkness surrounding me. I slid my hands into my pockets and kept my distance, watching her like a lost dog that'd just run away from her master.

Thirty seconds.

The lights from the city glowed like stars in the sky. She was absolutely silent as she stood there, and just as still. She didn't cower like prey, her body tall and strong as ever. Her shoulders were back, and she held herself with endless grace. Her chest slowly rose and fell.

Fifteen seconds.

I came closer to her, my hands steady. My heart was beating slowly, like the calm before the storm. While a hurricane swirled around us, the center was quiet and still. That was how we were—for now.

Five seconds.

I came up right behind her, my face almost touching

the back of her head. My hands stayed at my sides, and I resisted the urge to grab her. My knuckles ached to grip her hips, to pull her flush against me and make her mine.

Three.

Two.

One.

My watch beeped once from the timer I'd set.

It was done. She was officially mine.

"I knew you would be here…"

I pressed my lips to her ear, my hands moving to her hips. I finally got her in my grasp, felt her soft skin under my fingertips. I licked the shell of her ear before I spoke. "On. Your. Knees."

ALSO BY VICTORIA QUINN

The story continues in Boss Love.

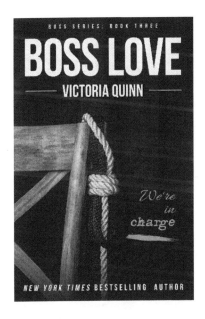

Order Now

Made in the USA
Middletown, DE
21 April 2020

89808097R00158